A QUEST FOR BEING

Larry D. Harwood
Illustrator: Elspeth Harwood

Cover image © Larry D. Harwood

www.innovativeinkpublishing.com
Send all inquiries to:
4050 Westmark Drive
Dubuque, IA 52004-1840

Print ISBN: 979-8-3851-1310-1
Ebook ISBN: 979-8-3851-1311-8

Published in the United States of America

For James and Samuel

"My days are like an evening shadow; I wither away like grass." Psalm 102:11

"O Lord, make me know my end and what is the measure of my days; let me know how fleeting I am! Behold, you have made my days a few hand-breadths, and my lifetime is as nothing before you." Psalm 39: 4-5

"For while we are still in this tent, we groan, being burdened—not that we would be unclothed, but that we would be further clothed, so that what is mortal may be swallowed up by life." 2 Corinthians 5: 4

Table of Contents

Preface

A few people have a mouse or two as pets, while most people disdain this rodent, particularly when these furry animals dare to steal into our dwellings and make themselves at home in what was previously *our* home. In the following story of animal adventure, mice are not villains, however, though they do occupy dwellings not their own. The intent of the tale in this book, wrapped around a single pair of mice, and eventually extended to a needy canine friend, points elsewhere. The migrating pair of wife Lilly and husband Geronimo Mouse are subject to a plethora of dangers due to the constraints of their species, and in competition with a host of larger and swifter animal predators and, of course, humans. The most notable liabilities of these creatures are an extremely short lifespan of a year or two and their small size. Nevertheless, the pair withstand an almost merciless vulnerability to stronger and vicious predators, while also befriending the canine Boris, who offers some aid to them and they to him.

By offering more than complaints when burdens arise, the humble Lilly Mouse, our story's patient heroine and caregiver, provides the reader an admirable example. She pushes forward to record her own tale of migration for her posterity, chronicling both joys and struggles of three creatures vying to make the most of their being together. By the end of a troubled but also rewarding adventure, the reader discovers why Lilly and Geronimo Mouse had to migrate from their original idyllic church home.

Larry D. Harwood
February 2024
La Crosse, Wisconsin

Acknowledgements

Kind thanks are extended to Carol Taylor for her evaluation of the manuscript of this book and for many helpful suggestions along the way. I also extend thanks to Lynnette Rogers, publishing supervisor at Innovative Ink, with whom I had my first conversation about the possibility of this book. To Angela Lampe, director of publishing at Innovative Ink, I am grateful for not a few encouraging conversations in every way needed to see this work to the end. Finally, to my wife Dottie I wish to express my sincere thanks for constant support for projects such as *A Quest for Being*. This project and others would have proved too formidable for me alone.

1

A pair of mice break up house

"I just heard something terrible," Geronimo Mouse explained to Lilly, who waited for more.

"Tell me," she responded, reaching to put her diary on the corner of the sofa.

"The few left voted to sell."

The time had come and Lilly's face registered shock, more than when the first rumors had surfaced.

"We'll have to move. Any buyer will push us off the grounds for sure, leastways out of the church."

"Is there another building for us?" she asked.

"I don't think any are suitable."

"And we were hoping to start our family here soon," she recalled, as tears now formed and rolled down her mouse cheeks.

"Lilly, we're still young. We can put off a family for a while yet. Right now we need another place. We can't delay. A new owner could be in here within a week."

"The trickle of people coming got smaller and smaller," she acknowledged, wiping her tears.

"Is there any wonder?" Geronimo responded. "We should have planned to leave before now," he continued. "I'll look for something else close by. Starting tomorrow is none too soon. While I'm out you get our things ready. Better to pack lightly. What you can get in a backpack for each of us. Truth be told, we've lived with too much ease here and we've been softened up.Our new life may be a hard one."

"Tomorrow you leave?" Lilly asked, stunned by the sudden turn of events.

"Before sunup," he answered. "For now, we'll have lunch. People will be out of the church afterward and we can move about then. We've not been outside this building in a while, so we'll take a little stroll—close to the structure, mind you. After dinner pack me a lunch for tomorrow if you will. I'll look for some maps."

Geronimo wiped Lilly's tear-stained cheeks, and the two set their table for Sunday lunch. The prayer before eating lasted longer than usual. All the same, the meal was pleasant, and as was his custom Geronimo complimented Lilly. Secretly, he wondered if Lilly and he would ever eat as well again, but resolutely dismissed that thought as he asked for more cranberries to go with the cheese. He did not see the usual Sunday chocolates, but said nothing.

The walk outside proved frightful and as scary as anything Lilly had witnessed since they had moved into the church house. Geronimo concealed his own fears, though he knew Lilly saw everything from winged predators to little to eat or drink. There was scarcely any tall grass for stealthy and safe movement, nor did the mice spot a single puddle of water anywhere for drink. Farther afield they did see what looked like greenery, maybe a garden; both remained unsure, for their mice eyes were not strong. After the few minutes of exposure to the great outdoors, Geronimo and Lilly fled back inside. The fright in Lilly's stomach showed on her face, and Geronimo quietly chastised himself for the two living like pampered church mice. His own stomach told him they were hardly prepared to face dangers, either small or large. Still, he resolved to face them for Lilly.

While Lilly made the single sandwich for his journey, Geronimo consulted the front pages of a phone book. One map included towns and regions beyond the immediate area, though Geronimo knew he could walk only a short distance in a single day. Sitting across the table from him, Lilly brushed away faint tears, as she got up to avoid his notice. Without trust in her husband's skill in meeting various dangers of the past, her tears might have turned into a flood.

Geronimo had spent three months in the Mouse Brigade, a fact which gave Lilly immense pride, especially as that amount of time was usually an eighth of a mouse's total life span. But for his chance meeting with Lilly the happy soldier might have made a career in the Brigade had not looks and words and finally love intruded. The couple afterward moved with the customary housing transitions mice are wont to make in their first days or weeks of marriage, all the time hoping for a housing arrangement beyond the temporary.

Since Geronimo was a reliable provider and protector from the start, Lilly had lived with few worries, and those only trivial, until the first rumors

that the congregation might fold and the church building be sold surfaced. The trek outside earlier had added fear and shook her remaining confidence about their future as much as the thought of now giving up the church house was painful. She shared Geronimo's worry that they had weakened their skills compared to those honed when life had been leaner and they in better form. The plentiful food from the church kitchen had loaded the two of them with extra weight that would certainly prove a handicap now. Lilly, however, knew Geronimo had little fear, for he knew that fears, warranted or unwarranted, must be restrained, and so he brooded over his maps, pointing to the paths to take, after asking Lilly to come back to the table. He sketched out a map for Lilly to follow his movements.

2

Geronimo goes on a reconnaissance mission and Lilly frets

Three hours before daybreak Lilly prepared breakfast for the two of them, though she ate little and offered her remainder to Geronimo. Into his backpack he placed his single sandwich and snacks of varied colors that Lilly always included with any lunch pack. He thanked her, but resisted Lilly's suggestion that he take a container filled with water, confident that there would be abundant ground pools he could drink from. Each kissed the other lightly on the cheek after an embrace, and then without fanfare Geronimo vanished into the dark. Lilly sat down only for a moment before beginning to busy herself with worries and stared at how little she could cram into two backpacks, until gripping fear for Geronimo's safety overpowered other worries. Still, she had confidence in her husband, though maybe more than she should, she suspected.Meanwhile, her frequent repose in Geronimo in the coming weeks would serve them well, until he began to show himself as fragile as any other mouse. To Lilly, for now, he was exemplary, something she had known from the first time her tiny eyes had spotted the majestic mouse nine weeks earlier. In fact, when she glimpsed him, she said—though only to herself—"This is him." He had greeted the stranger with a friendly smile and had asked her to sit down beside him on a large rock. Why he expressed so much interest in her she had only a faint inkling at the time, until she found the courage to ask him days later, after he had proposed marriage to her.

"You were irresistibly attractive and a good conversationalist, once I got you to talk," he had responded, and she had blushed.

Truth was, she thought he her better in both categories, and for as long as he didn't seem to mind, neither would she. Her relatives, soon meeting this likely groom, quickly came to like, and even more, respect Geronimo. The life of the couple after marriage soon plummeted into tragedy as an epidemic of tick fever began to drastically reduce the numbers of their extended family. Nevertheless, as death reigned for some days, survivors amongst this mice family remained aware of the habitual hardships of life, even death, so wiped their brows and kept their faces forward. Of Geronimo's seven siblings, only one survived the epidemic—Maverick. After the death of their siblings the two brothers promised more time with one another. Geronimo had always enjoyed his younger brother's company, for both of them were mechanically minded and always, separately and together, at work on some gadget of body protection for vulnerable mice.

Death for mice came not only by sickness, for if there was one unbendable rule for safeguarding mouse safety, it was that no mouse should ever initiate any words with a human until the human first made strong and then unmistakable overtures in the direction of friendliness. A mouse aspiring to communication must wait for an opportunity that might reveal an actual invitation to the mouse. At the church house no such opportunities had come for Lilly and Geronimo Mouse. All told, however, in most every other respect their environment and life at the church had been idyllic. As brief tenants at one other property before the church house, and much different from the church, Geronimo and Lilly enjoyed amicable relationships with the owners, though the physical properties themselves were squalid. Hostile cats, too, presented perennial dangers for the two mice, until the incensed owners rebuked the two offending felines, contrary to the usual behavior of most house owners, who almost always favored their cats over mice. The pair of mice soon were of a mind to never leave the house in hopes of anything better. However, after two electrical fires, Geronimo had insisted they move. He was right. Only a week later, with a third fire, the house burned to the ground. The resident couple had not been home. The whereabouts and fates of the two villainous felines remained unknown. Wanting to avoid the impression of any pleasure in the likely deaths of the two felines, the mouse couple simply said nothing, except both knew that with virtually nine lives promised a cat, this death, even if actual, left eight more tries. "Would that we had that much extension," Geronimo mused.

With marital remembrances of her and Geronimo swirling about in her head, Lilly lay down for a rest, but badgering worry for Geronimo prevented any sleep. Getting up, she made a sandwich just like the one she had prepared for Geronimo the night before. Thoughts for Geronimo's safety intruded again, so she put away her sandwich and brought out *I Climbed a Mountain*, but she first recorded in her diary what had happened the previous day, as unsettling as it was. After some tears moistened her careful lettering, she put the diary away, but her favorite book remained on her lap.

The thought that she could become a widow at any minute, or perhaps already was one, stole into her mind, scuttling more pleasant remembrances. Despite Geronimo's warning that morning against her venturing outside on her own, she hastily improvised a plan and laced up her boots, ready to go outside and welcome Geronimo back, should he return early. After a string of doubts almost turned her from this unwise venture, she nevertheless decided this was no time to question her own decision and stood up in her boots. Hardly aware of what should happen next, she began shouting orders to herself for getting to the door. On went a visor hat to keep her face partially hidden from winged enemies.

Outside, Lilly trembled in her boots when an eager hawk spotted her, and she had no sooner heard the frightful wings in motion than she scrambled back into the safety of the church. Now resolved that this was no time for tears, she endeavored to try packing again. If Geronimo found his Lilly gone on his return, it would be devastation enough to make even a strong mouse weak. She must try again for sterner stuff in herself.

3

Lilly waits out the night alone

The afternoon and then evening dragged on. She remembered that since their wedding they had hardly been out of each other's sight more than a very few minutes. Such a thought hardly gave hope now, given that her hardy and savvy Geronimo might be no more. Such thoughts she must put away for good. Per his request she had made Geronimo neither sandwich nor snack for supper. When suppertime came she ate alone, as he had insisted she should that morning, if he had not returned by then. He might possibly turn up by dusk, but if not, she ought not panic nor assume the worst; extra time and tardiness might indicate more promise than peril, perhaps even that he had found a living space requiring more studied investigation before returning. How she envied humans their telephones and not just their cars, as Geronimo sometimes did. She must agonize until her only news came with his return—if he returned. She must be made of stronger stuff, she told herself again, after this reflection.

Between them only Geronimo had had a conversation with a human. The two mice were schooled in some of the writings of humans and came from families insisting upon this in their offspring. After reading, speaking the language was the next desired skill level, asonly a very few in the mouse world had mastered it. Geronimo had managed to achieve a level of near fluency while Lilly had gained a more modest facility in this most envied skill of the mouse world. Naturally, if a mouse was to converse with a human, however rarely opportunity arose, possession of this skill was mandatory. Lacking it, a human could put a cornered mouse into a frighteningly perilous situation. The registry of short-lived mice dead by violence was high.

A church house creaks a lot at night, when temperatures start to descend from warmer daytime readings, but neither darkness nor cool air had previously presented much obstacle to these mice. The two rarely felt the need to exercise anything more than prudence within their living space, and they only rarely left their domicile at the church house.

Given the need to meticulously scrutinize any potential living space, Geronimo might need another day, at least part of a second day, to assess as much as he could. Rare it was that a mouse habitat provided security enough to give sustaining confidence to mouse residents. Their church house was almost one of a preferred kind, for some and even most homes of mice were full of lurking dangers, generally requiring that one member of the resident mice always be on guard for their safety. Some habitations were either tremendously cold or tremendously hot. Their church house provided heating in winter and conditioned air in summer. Some residences were close to food resources and others not. Their church house quarters were only a few feet from the church kitchen. Though very few, occasionally a place to stay came with friendly cats. A component of the very best places to live, such as their church house—came with no cats at all.

These considerations of a paradise about to be lost hardly consoled this troubled mouse, as she changed into night clothes and prepared for a sleep she suspected would be without Geronimo. She could manage one night without him, she assured herself. Her husband cared for her in a way she treasured, though she always kept the thought to herself, for it was considered uncouth in mouse culture to boast, even if the boast rang true.

4

A battered Geronimo returns home

Darkened blood dropped across the floor the next morning as Lilly dragged the resistant body across the tiles. Without any aid she heaved Geronimo up onto the coach.

"I'm okay," he quipped.

"I see," Lilly affirmed, though she did not, but vowed to herself to ask no questions. For a husband who had endured heavens knows what, she would not ask him to recount a bloody confrontation and maybe more than one. At least he had made it back to the church house, she told herself.

"Did you manage any sleep?" she asked anyway.

"No."

"Not a bit?"

"Don't think so. My hurts aren't that serious," he protested. "A hawk dropped me about fifty feet up. If I hadn't landed in branches, the bare ground would have done me in and the hawk would have had a helpless mouse to eat on the ground."

"How did you get down?

"Can't say. That part is a blur now; maybe humans aren't the only species with adrenalin."

"I can patch you up for us to leave?" Lilly asked, as she tried to make her words not sound like a question.

"If you can patch me up enough to go again. We don't have much time. Did you see the sale sign already?"

She dared not tell him about her misadventure outside.

"No," she said, though now remembering she had.

"Let's plan for a couple days here before we go. I hope no more," Geronimo said, and turned his bloodied face to her.

"Looks like you've got most everything ready," he added, with a smile that revealed his pain.

"What do we do with what's left? It's not a little."

"We may come back for it. I wish we could have stayed here too, Lilly, but every light went out of this place," Geronimo said.

"It would be nice to find another church house," Lilly offered, but Geronimo said nothing more and Lilly immediately regretted her words. She would focus on her injured husband.

5

Good books are good medicine

Determining that three of his thirteen ribs had suffered cracks, Lilly insist-ed that Geronimo take three days of rest before another night venture. Both would spend that time in reading, for theirs was not only a literate household, but one given to some knowledge of the world afield.Being the small creatures they were, they could hardly "see the world" as they heard humans refer to expensive vacations and trips to foreign and exotic places. With the obstacles of a short lifespan and extremely limited means of travel, Lilly and Geronimo Mouse had given themselves the next best thing—books. Not all mice, howev-er, had a desire to read books, or to acquire learning from books, which mice of this sort contemptuously referred to, as useless "book learning." This mock-ing phrase some mice had picked up from human counterparts who shared a low estimation of books, and indeed of knowledge itself.

Lilly and Geronimo Mouse refused to share in a contempt for learning. When the couple required physical or psychic energy they habitually turned to reading, and frequently to books already read more than a few times. So, while Geronimo recovered he insisted that they reread two of their favorites, books considered masterpieces of mouse fictional literature. He had no need to persuade Lilly. Just as much as hilarity was a main part of the stories, so too examples of courage occupied virtually every page. Though the inevitable laughter that would come with this reading would irritate and upset the three cracked ribs of Geronimo, he would endure for the larger pleasure of enjoying the tales again.[1]

---

1. One of the books read was *I Climbed a Mountain*, written by the most famous mountain climber in all of mousedom. This hardy individual dared to defy all odds mental and material stacked against such a small creature as himself, and so was held up as something of a mythical hero in mouse histo-ry. Particulars included scaling a peak so high that it took him forty-six years—well over twenty or so

A book different from *I Climbed a Mountain*, but virtually identical in moral injunctions with a summons to courage was *Pass me the Cheese, and Start with the Feta.*[2]

"So when do we make our move again?" Lilly asked Geronimo after three days of rest and reading.

"How about tomorrow after dusk?" he answered.

"So it is," she smiled. "That will give you almost another day to rest."

---

times the normal lifetime of an average mouse—to reach the summit, though it only took thirty-seven years for his descent. The fortitude and resolve of this mountain climber was evident on every page and the story full of laughter and mischief. It ends with the woes this famous man encountered from his own relatives, when he should have been honored by them.

2. This masterpiece was subtly presented as a book of instruction in mouse culinary arts that a substantial number of kitchens in mice households near and far in time studied for its appetizing recipes for ripening cheeses and detailed instruction on how to ingest this meal staple of mice, to the point of never leaving the table. Naturally nutritionists and dieticians and the whole segment of people counting themselves health experts despised and opposed the book, from the very beginning. To these critics, if food caused the eater to want more food, then that was something the experts could not approve. The author quickly became a symbol of fortitude among most mice, for this author turned on his critics and castigated them as reprehensible food police. Humiliated, the critics made a hasty retreat from the public eye to the ivory tower where the book's fans hoped they would stay, threatening to pummel them with rotting tomatoes—but not good cheese of any kind—if they did not. When a couple misguided souls did try for about a year to relaunch the prior criticism of the book, the reading public's patience quickly grew thin with these pompous experts. In fact, the author himself sent the two food "experts" a collector's copy of *I Climbed a Mountain* and scribbled on the inside the suggestion that both men undertake such a journey as had Ephraim Mouse, author of *I Climbed a Mountain*, with the caveat that the two try for a lengthier stay than the author of that work so they would never be seen again.

6

An aborted night journey brings Lilly and Geronimo back home

Less than an hour into their evening journey the next day, thunder cracked overhead before a downpour descended on the pair and sent them scurrying for cover. Geronimo wrapped some small bush branches together with his default rubber bands to provide a canopy of leaves above, with a low side where most of the water scooted off. Still not done, the military mouse trained in survival scrounged for and eventually found some dry field grass for a warm but mostly comforting fire. He even pulled a poncho from his back pack and with help from Lilly managed to cover the top of the bush with more than leafy branches.

"I think we best spend our night here," Geronimo suggested to Lilly, after the second hour of unrelenting rain. She reached into her backpack for sleepers for each of them.

"One of the comforts of home," she said and smiled at Geronimo. He later shared recollections from *I Climbed a Mountain*, but then they kissed each other good night before falling asleep. It was two hours before midnight. Probably no other mouse couple enjoyed as much indifference to a downpour of rain as did Lilly and Geronimo in their temporary felicity before their sleep was interrupted.

"Lilly, Lilly!" Geronimo shouted as loud as he dared.

The gurgling sound of water tripping over stones in the field and the pounding rain roused Lilly as the quick Geronimo waited for her to slide out and then reached over her to shove her sleeper into her backpack after packing his own away.

"It's only rainwater," he announced.

"And plenty of it," Lilly concurred.

"We'll have to detour to avoid the highest water," he said, as the two now took flight across a field softened to mussiness by the downpour. Every twenty feet or so they forded another stream of runoff, as Geronimo worried what they might do with a body of water too large to cross.

"I think we must turn around," he confessed.

"Turn around?" she asked.

"The field and gullies to cross every few feet will defeat us," Geronimo said, wiping the water off his face.

"What about our plan!" she objected.

"We'll recast our plan in the morning.We're making no progress to our destination like this."

"We go back to the bush?"

"No. We're maybe less than an hour from the church house."

"Back home?"

"I think so. If you are agreeable," he said.

"I suppose so," Lilly agreed, actually quietly overjoyed that the two would enjoy the comforts of their old home once more, even if their journey had stalled so soon.

"We'll dry out and check the weather forecast before we leave again," Geronimo offered.

The downpour increased as they traversed backwards to the church house. This time Lilly did not mind wading through streams as she would welcome exchanging her soaked clothes for dry ones. She held Geronimo's warm hand, not a tad cold, in the chilly rain.

After four hours of sleep on the bare but dry floor of the church house, the morning sun woke them. The cheeses they had taken on the trek remained edible and the strawberries, though soft, still appetizing. Lilly insisted on making a pot of coffee. The previous evening when they left both had had a strong cup before.

That afternoon Geronimo studied the anticipated weather from newspapers found in the church office, and Lilly set about cleaning muddy clothes and shoes before she packed food for their next journey.

7

Two mice enjoy some comforts before returning to the world outside

Lilly had made their living quarters in the church house as comfortable as any residence any mouse ever called home. Even after her earlier packing, and with much removed, their forlorn quarters still had a look of friendly invitation. Tears Lilly preferred Geronimo not see welled up in her eyes as happy memories of their church house quarters filled her thoughts, as the two tried to keep their focus on the coming migration. Geronimo dropped a model car tiny enough for his pocket into a back pocket, but not before he held the lacquered item before Lilly, who smiled.

The bed, taken apart earlier by Geronimo, had remained disassembled on the floor. When Lilly saw Geronimo unrolling a blanket to make a bed, she followed suit and pushed her own blanket close to him. She suspected that returning to a home you had loved precluded any feeling of glee, for it could only be fleeting. After a while, however, she recognized her musings came from self-pity, so she stopped and resolutely wiped her cheeks and reached over and kissed the already asleep Geronimo, though having forgotten her diary she quietly got up. She stood as she wrote, while Geronimo never moved, and so she went a bit longer and then tucked the diary back into her backpack.

Tomorrow would be another day, and she would do her part in making it a better one.

8

A near-death experience
on the high seas

"Geronimo, where is the bridge!"

"The deluge took it out?" Geronimo reasoned, as taken aback as Lilly.

"Can we cross somewhere else?" Lilly asked.

"We'll have to. Too risky to cross here and especially right now. I mean in the dark," Geronimo added.

"We wait for daybreak?" Lilly asked. "Couldn't we have done that back at the church house?" she inquired.

"We won't make it in flood waters in the dark. We'll have a better chance when the sun comes up. Our eyes aren't the best you know."

"A chance?" Lilly muttered under her breath. "Sorry," she blurted out. Geronimo did not hear any of her words.

"We'll need some daylight before we dare cross this water. It'll be hard enough even then," Geronimo admitted, looking up at Lilly after he stared at the wet ground. Lilly thought of the floor at the church house and how she preferred it to this body of water.

"I'm not a soldier in your army," she said and loud enough this time for Geronimo to hear.

"Let's try for some sleep until daylight," he offered.

She tried hard not to grimace, and then realized the two of them might have just had their first argument. He began to gather stubble and leaves to make for some cushion beneath their sleepers and after a few seconds of pause, Lilly proceeded to help. She tried hard to smile now as Geronimo helped her into her sleeper and then he went to work on putting a poncho over shrub limbs again for some deflection of the falling rain. He reached over after that and quietly kissed Lilly's cheek.

Four hours later Geronimo woke Lilly from their bed on the wet ground.

"Time to swim," he said.

Lilly rubbed her eyes, changed into her day clothes and then rolled up their sleepers, pushing both down into her husband's backpack. Lilly saw that he had packed more of her stuff into his.

"You'll do this, Lilly?" he asked.

She nodded, a little ashamed of her earlier hesitations.

"There's a lumber mill up the hill. The wood chips on the ground came from there and I need one a little bigger than what I've found," Geronimo explained.

"How big?" Lilly asked.

"Long as we are tall and only as wide as our waists are narrow."

Lilly had hardly imagined that her husband, with her in tow, planned for the pair to cross the river lying horizontally on a skimpy plank no wider nor longer than their flesh. After more searching the ground, Geronimo found his boat; it appeared as narrow as the two of them.

"And how does this work?" Lilly inquired, part of her fear now subdued by her curiosity. She forced on herself renewed trust in Geronimo.

"You'll lie on top of me, and we'll paddle with our arms when we hit water. Where we're at, the water moves quickly, but there's a bend in the river a few feet that way, slowing it. Still it will push us hard downstream as we try for sideways. Our trip should take us about three, maybe four minutes to reach the bank, if all goes right. Paddle as hard as you can; getting to the bank and not further downstream will depend on our quickness. The faster we get there, the quicker we're out of danger here and can be on our way!"

Her husband said nothing more, or at least nothing Lilly heard.Her arms wrapped around Geronimo and Geronimo strapped to the piece of wood from his shoulders to his ankles, he walked with a stilted and jerky gait, though without hesitation, toward the water. Lilly now placed her arms more tightly around him and on Geronimo's shrill count of three the pair fell forward, sandwiched together. Hitting the water stunned both, but Lilly's body hardly shifted from atop her husband's body, now underneath the surface, as she and Geronimo immediately rotated their arms in propelling fashion, like tiny though sturdy waterwheels.

Geronimo's plan suddenly went awry as the colossal mouth of a hungry lunker scooped the entire female mouse body up and off Geronimo and then

shut his fish mouth. From below Geronimo felt the fish's slick underbelly as it snatched Lilly from him.

Lilly vanished into the aquatic beast, while Geronimo shoved himself toward the river bank, now only a few feet away. Finally clawing his way up the muddy bank and then loosening his ropes, he fell face down on the wet ground, weeping without pause for the absent Lilly. He had never until this moment spent a second of his married life contemplating what his life might be without her.Now he had no reason to make his way to a new home; instead he could resign himself to live as a coarse field mouse and forget past domestic felicity with Lilly.

These despairing thoughts vanished when Geronimo spotted a bedraggled and bloodied Lilly climbing up out of the water.

9

Recovery from near death
and disaster

Lilly's face showed two vertical scars, neither very deep and both distant enough from her eyes to not jeopardize already weak mouse vision. Other and plentiful scratches showed across the back of her legs, with trousers cut into dangling strips of material, making her resemble an outfitted circus animal they had witnessed in an adjacent town, when hiding under bleacher seats.

Geronimo scarcely took his hands off Lilly for an hour while they found a shrub to cuddle beneath and, interspersed with careful hugs and kisses, recounted the nearly deadly disaster.

"I saw you put that it in your pocket and figured you intended it for me," she explained.

"You understood, then," Geronimo affirmed, as he gently rubbed her wet mouse hair on a scratched arm.

"When we shoved off I grabbed it immediately. I popped it in my mouth, clamped it between my teeth. It was so repulsive in odor and taste I wanted to spit it out, but I knew not to. When the fish took me for a ride, I spit the putrid thing out and figured it would do the trick on him. I stayed in his mouth no more than five or so seconds, not even enough time to get acquainted. He spit me out and I didn't see him anymore."

The mental and physical exhaustion of both mice prevented further journey toward the junk yard of which Lilly had heard nothing yet from Geronimo, while the rest of the day they ate the sandwiches Lilly had made. Items in their backpacks had suffered in fording the river, but the afternoon sun dried most.

23

Lilly adored fine things, fine literature, and a fine living space, and Geronimo knew he had no fine dwelling to offer his mate within the next few hours, as renewed worry over the decrepit living space in the junkyard he had found days before infiltrated his thoughts.

Geronimo had no intention of making any kind of permanent home sandwiched in a junk yard between other mangled and wrecked cars. The yard would provide a temporary residence. However, what Lilly might think on seeing contorted and rusty car bodies abandoned because the heaps had no other home, he feared to guess. Indeed, four nights ago the yard had presented a ghastly picture of vehicular death with rows of silent automobiles. These were haphazardly stored and encroaching weeds pushed against car window glass while other weeds climbed lazily through the opening of missing windshields.

Geronimo determined to banish such thoughts, if he could. For now overwhelming relief that Lilly had come back from nearly certain death in her harrowing ordeal with the jaws of a fish kept worse thoughts at bay. He could swell with pride that she had won the uneven battle with such an unequal adversary and that she exhibited little evidence of shell-shock after her brush with death. Geronimo had every reason to be overjoyed and would now force himself to think on these things for as long as he could. The junkyard they would deal with later, all other things being equal, for the two had life ahead of them, however brief.

Lilly did not remain unruffled by escaping from a death too horrible to imagine, and she vowed to herself to record such an experience for her posterity. Up until now, her diary had mostly captured ordinary tales. Today gave occasion to recount her own near-death in ink and not in blood. Happy and overjoyed she should be.

10

A new home is accepted by Lilly

The adaptability with which mice must live their lives to maintain a frequently threatened existence constantly required attention to means of survival. Even in the same general vicinity, variation among landscapes and larger environments presented seemingly infinite dangers, requiring unflinching alertness. Mouse housing varied from packed earth to posh penthouse living on the fortieth or higher floor of an urban skyscraper. Usually, the more desirable the living space, the more dangerous, as it also brought larger human populations. Nevertheless, even the most primitive mouse quarters, while buffered from some of the dangers of modern urban life, presented hazards that lurked in and around the soil, water, mud, or straw. Indeed, a city mouse exposed for the first time to the wilds of nature and the lethal terrors of a rural environment would often panic at the first sight of danger and turn tail and run.

"What is that?" Lilly asked.

Geronimo's heart sank as he stopped in his tracks and threw away his crafted but unspoken explanation, painfully composed in the past hour. He would leave Lilly's question unanswered for a few seemingly eternal seconds as he now surveyed the mass of automobile wrecks in daylight.

"No houses around," Lilly observed, neither of the two looking at the other while staring at the wasteland of wrecks.

"We're on the edge of a little village here," Geronimo began. "There are some dwellings as you get closer to the center," he continued. "Lilly . . . ," he started to say, but he managed no more words. After a few more seconds, he started again.

"When I came here, four days ago now, I found no access to any house we might desire, though I figured the village must have a church, maybe even more than one. But I didn't see any."

"So what did you find?" Lilly asked, without any tone of impatience in her words.

He would delay his answer and explanation no longer.

"Lilly, this is what I found," he said as shame welled up in Geronimo Mouse's face and he turned away. He stared blankly at the monotonous rows of automobile wrecks imprisoned behind a diamond patterned fence that at least permitted mice easy entry.

"You did pick one for us?" she asked.

Geronimo looked up and wiped his face.

"Well, yes. I found three that are suitable I think. The three are all red."

"Red I do prefer."

"That I knew," Geronimo said, and for the first time in the past hour he managed a faint smile. Geronimo now suspected his worries had been ex-

cessive, and he moved to plant a cautious kiss on a bruised and swollen face. Lilly gave Geronimo a studied look, almost like an adoring pupil looks at her teacher as a fount of wisdom, something Geronimo knew he hardly possessed. Rather, in his view, though unspoken, Lilly was that.

"We mice can live luxurious lives, but we know how to get on, even when it means learning to live in a junkyard in a wrecked car for a while," Lilly said, smiling a little as she selected her words.

"Only for a while," Geronimo insisted, as the abiding thoughts and scare of her near-death earlier that morning prevented more joy. Choosing in a junkyard a temporary living space was no insurmountable task, for above all things a mouse must be adaptable and his wife Lilly appeared that. Now he smiled.

"If Ephraim Mouse had pondered too much over that monstrous mountain in front of him," she started, "he would never had made the first step. If he had quibbled with the giant mountain beforehand, he would be unknown to posterity, after bemoaning his task as impossible before he even started. He would probably eventually have crawled home if he could have even remembered where home was." Lilly never let an opportunity pass to praise the famous mouse of legend.

"Leastways this junkyard is mostly flat, and not a mountain reaching into the sky, like Ephraim found his mountain to be," Geronimo added.

Lilly laughed a little.

"Most people think these places are unsightly. Sometimes neighbors complain and owners put a screening fence around these eyesores. Looks like that's what they've tried to do here," Geronimo said, as dusk approached.

Lilly had fallen asleep and collapsed to the ground, Geronimo presumed from exhaustion. He picked her up and carried her to a junked automobile.

11

A canine makes himself known to his visitors

"Where did you get the water?" she inquired the next morning at about the time they liked to take breakfast when they lived in the church house. She rubbed her eyes ever so gently with her question.

"I had to fight a mongrel for it!" Geronimo responded.

"A dog?"

"Not just any dog. This one makes a bad dog look angelic. A junkyard dog he is and he's ornery."

"And how did you deal with this mongrel?" Lilly asked.

"I tried to negotiate with the beast, but nothing doing."

"What happened?"

"I found one water puddle in here, but close to him, and he refused to share, even though I spotted his water bowl. I had sneaked up from behind, but he smelled me and came at me."

"So what happened then?"

"The puddle lay within easy reach of his chain, so I couldn't get to the water without confronting him."

"But you still got the water?"

"I pulled a trick on him."

"Tell me."

"I told him that we mice may not come off as strong, but I'd seen pebbles lying around and I could toss them into his water puddle, hardly any size at all, till all the water splashed out and then he'd have no water to drink, not for a while anyway. Meanwhile, I pretended not to notice his water bowl. It sat full of water, though what looked like his food bowl sat empty. "

"So what did he say?"

"Just scowled resentfully that he lived on a chain, but boasted he could yank the chain out of the ground to easily get me if he wanted, so I of course didn't let my guard down for a second. I told him I had a small bottle and needed to fill it for you. He tipped his head slightly as if to say go ahead, and I did. Said he wouldn't think of providing bread or water for his mate, or ex-mate, and wondered why I would. I gave him no answer. I never took my eyes off of him, partly because his teeth looked larger than those of any river fish I could imagine. Sure enough, when I had the bottle about half full, he made his lunge at me, deciding he had been too generous, I guess."

"But the bottle was full?" Lilly puzzled.

"Yeah, on the way back here I discovered another water puddle, so I finished filling it there. I don't have to deal with that wretch again, not for a while anyway," Geronimo pronounced.

"And he didn't get any of you when he went at you?"

"Just the end of my tail, nothing more," Geronimo boasted, while Lilly made him turn around to see how much was missing. He indicated no pain and instead insisted that he would not require as much at feeding times anymore.

Lilly smiled and focused her eyes, while Geronimo ferreted out the very last of yesterday's sandwiches and remaining pieces of cheese. When they had finished, Geronimo straightened their blanket for the back seat of the car, which was in remarkably good shape. It had provided plenty of sleeping room the previous night.

"Later we'll look at some other wrecks," he suggested.

Lilly nodded but fell back onto the blanket asleep. Geronimo surveyed the trunk, the lid open enough to investigate inside. Anything that might have been a front seat was slammed into the dash with no intervening space remaining. Lilly would hopefully not ask about the wreck. He did not want to describe a death by automobile when she had come so close to her own practically on the same day.

12

Geronimo reveals an unfulfilled love of automobiles

Geronimo possessed a fascination with cars, not watches, not fishing lures, not compasses, and Lilly knew this. In the human world of invention, Geronimo counted automobiles the most enthralling pieces of machinery ever fashioned. Fuming that mice were hardly fitted in physique to drive, he still dreamed of getting this mechanical marvel to respond to his hands and feet. Denial of this dream seemed to him one of the greatest deprivations of mouse existence, leastways for male mice. Often with both a dropped jaw and acute envy Geronimo noted the leisured mode with which drivers undertook their task. In warm weather, drivers would typically place their left arm on the car door in a relaxed carefree fashion as if attention were hardly required for a machine that appeared to virtually drive itself. Everything about the experience suggested this event one of the most satisfying of all human experiences, exempting of course, familial relationships and shared intimacies, he said to himself.Geronimo's dream of such an idyllic experience with these machines was interrupted when Lilly called him back to make the choice of which wreck should be their temporary residence.

"One of the red ones?" Lilly offered.

"How about the 1948 Ford coupe down this row?" Geronimo tossed out to Lilly, with no inkling that this vehicle would later transport him and Lilly out of this wasteland of wrecked automobiles.

"Quite all right by me," she said, "though its blue, not red. More important for now is we need something to eat," she smiled, getting off the subject of automobiles.

"The humans that run this place got food somewhere inside, I'll bet. Maybe that impolite dog can offer something," Geronimo scoffed. He found himself still smarting from the incident with the beast only minutes earlier.

13

Mice are unwelcome and on the run

The voice of a worker inside the building did nothing to quieten the barking mongrel. Remembering and fuming over the earlier vanity of the beast, Geronimo positioned himself with Lilly where the incensed dog saw both unwelcome mice, as the commanding voice in the building continued to no avail the effort to silence the barking animal. Geronimo now made false feints toward the beast while Lilly, encouraged to the point of boldness, stood up on her back legs to further agitate the mutt. The adrenalized dog charged toward Lilly as Geronimo calmly watched. Confident Lilly could manage the brute on her own, he turned his thoughts to investigating the inviting canteen he had spotted in a corner of the building.

With more appetite for food than bawdy entertainment with an ill-tempered dog, Geronimo darted into the building in full view of the agitated animal. Soon tired of any further games with the dog, Lilly raced into the building and joined Geronimo in hiding behind two shovels leaned against the inside wall. Within seconds the pair panicked when Geronimo brushed against the propped shovels and sent one and then both handles crashing to the concrete and grease-stained floor. Not sure they had given away their location, the two mice nevertheless feared to remain frozen, and in panic, sprinted out into the open—in full view of clearly unfriendly humans! Confrontation with the mongrel they had expected, but they froze with fright as the two yard workers now gave full chase to the shaking rodent pair.

To survive danger, mice must master the art of avoiding detection, especially when vulnerability comes so quickly that a mouse has almost literally no time to form an adequate defense while his life hangs in the balance. In such a situation an adversary may be as close as one human arm's length and may-

be even closer. If an actual confrontation is imminent, the cornered mouse can run swiftly through the legs of his confronter. Depending on the agility and physical speed of a pursuer, this single defensive maneuver skillfully employed can provide superb advantage over an opponent sufficient for the targeted animal to survive a close encounter. If the mouse's pursuer has the liability of weightiness, then the much smaller but agile mouse simply repeats his maddening maneuver of an exhausting rapid- motion-hide-and-seek over and over. Eventually his pursuer is so overcome with dizziness from all the swirling in opposite directions that he becomes breathless and hence gives up any further effort to capture or harm his opponent. The mouse has thereby tricked his pursuer into a ploy so exhausting that in no time at all the assailant passes out from sheer exhaustion and thereby concedes victory to the mouse by giving up the chase. Usually, however, a keener pursuer is not so easily thwarted by confusing the direction he should go to achieve his goal of a captured mouse. When a mouse runs under and through a set of human legs joined to a human brain, an extra tactic must follow for the mouse faced by such an opponent. Nevertheless, when the cringing mouse has little or no time to think, and lacks any sophisticated plan, he can probably evade capture by the simple ploy described here.

14

The canine and Lilly enter into negotiations

Plans to invade the inviting canteen were delayed when the two men brandished the downed shovels against the tiny intruders. Taking hasty flight and ducking down, they slid beneath the humming drink machine in the canteen corner. Neither pursuer had seen where the two disappeared, and the two men now fought over who bore responsibility for ignorance of the whereabouts of the culprits. Safe for the moment, Geronimo instructed Lilly to venture back to the '48 Ford by skirting the outside of the building, and to wait for him in the Ford. Before leaving the building, he would pick up a stash of edibles from the canteen. He offered a quick smile to Lilly. Meanwhile, Lilly's trust in his expertise with such tactics provoked her again to marveling, even in the heat of conflict with large adversaries. Renewed confidence in herself, exhibited in her mocking dance staged before the mongrel only minutes earlier, made her virtually ready to do most anything to secure the meal that her husband would soon provide. Her only regret for the moment was that Geronimo would be left to fight the fight, while she would have the solace of returning to the car and waiting for her hero.

"We'll eat when I come out of here with the food," he said to Lilly, as he kissed her lightly on the cheek. While Geronimo for the time being remained hidden from their two pursuers, Lilly now stepped out into the open and waited for the two men to catch sight of her. She threw her tail up in the air again, just as she had done with the mutt outside, and within seconds the two men were pointing and shouting while running in her direction. Lilly suddenly felt a surge of pride in her new abilities and thankfulness to Geronimo for his confidence in her.

She found a bent side door to slip through that proved easy enough for a slender mouse, but in the next instant her expectation of success suffered near destruction when the yard dog suddenly appeared and lunged at her, his mouth dripping saliva. Her short mouse hairs stood straight up and probably turned gray, though only temporarily. With hope for their future as dead as she might be shortly, she fell prostrate before the brute with no hope of saving herself.

"I can make a deal," she screeched, nevertheless.

"Better than that skimpy carcass you're showing?" the saliva-dripping dog retorted, as he flashed his enormous teeth with an unfriendly grin. For the moment it seemed the dog would refuse to broker any deal with the cornered weakling mouse until she discovered his weakness, or rather, his appetite.

"My husband—"

"Yeah, yeah. I met him already and the scrawny specimen tricked me, twice—and the last time with you joining in the shenanigans," the beast said, anxious to eat, and not talk. "And you mocked me with that scrawny tail, not ten minutes," he charged. "I can take some of it off you, like I did to your husband."

"He'll be coming out of the canteen shortly with all the food he can carry." Lilly tried to speak her words without jitters in her voice.

"He's a scrawny mouse, like you," the dog charged, indignant that this mouse might think him stupidly swayable.

"You're eating well enough? I mean, you don't need a little more?" Lilly asked.

"I get barely enough. That tree you almost ran into—it provides some rotten apples I gather up in the evenings after I'm let loose. Paltry stuff it is. I haven't had a hot dog, just a piece of one, mind you, since yesterday. They think it makes me meaner to starve me."

"We must hurry! You protect me, and you get half the food my husband brings out of that building later. No tricks—promise!"

The dog tried to look uninterested. Finally, he broke. "A whole hot dog?"

"They are in the canteen?"

"Oh yeah, they're always there, but rarely for me," he complained, "Not until Adam took over this place, did I ever even get any," he added.

"Okay," she answered, and hearing the shouting men coming closer, Lilly went for broke: "Dog, I'm not running from you. You either hide me under one those monster paws of yours or you gobble me up right here and now," Lilly shouted, as loud as a mouse voice could shout, while remaining hopeful the dog would take the option she preferred. "That hot dog will taste better than me," she added. "Besides, we mice carry a lot of irksome parasites within these mortal bodies that you probably don't want to sponsor." She did not mention to her adversary that she and Geronimo had regular flushings at a clinic run by a mouse friend. A look of horror came over the brute's face. Lilly figured that maybe she had just saved her life.

15

The canine suffers rebukes
by his employers

Two empty-handed and humiliated men, outfoxed by two tiny rodents, now ran from the building and out to the dog, who refused to get up for them and instead began his deep and thunderous bark. The two had by now given up any effort to apprehend the mice and instead decided to rebuke the dog for his incessant barking. The dog did not flinch or move, despite them, except when he lunged straight at them once without warning, and one of the men fell backwards.

"Lazy animal, except when he barks!" the downed worker shouted, while the other nodded his head in agreement. The dog meanwhile erupted with renewed barking, vicious-sounding and loud enough that the two men retreated, fearing the animal might spring from his haunches for real. The dog sat back on his hind feet instead, laughing to himself that he could provoke these two into cowardly fear, even as their insults continued, though now at a safe distance.

"We need another dog, not this good-for-nothing beast. One capable of at least smelling out some mice!" the worst critic of the mongrel complained, as the two men, disgusted, turned and headed back toward the building, but not before spitting on the ground close to him, hastening away to show their displeasures, as well as their humiliation.

"I didn't know if my paw would cover you," the dog said to Lilly after the men were out of earshot, though the two still hurled insults at the dog as they sauntered back into the building.

"It pays to be small on occasion," Lilly said to the beast, still gasping for breath after the weight of the dog's back foot lifted and she could take in fresh air again. "My tail was still a quarter out, so I feared they might spot it and I'd suffer for it."

"Truth is, they're not so bright," the beast asserted, in a simple matter-of-fact voice.

"Thank you for what you did," Lilly said, and the dog tipped his head.She was grateful but still cautious toward an animal that minutes earlier had confronted her as his prey.

"I stage an act like that once in a while. Can't let them think me soft or incapable. If they did, they'd give me my pink slip for sure. Once in a while, they need to see a real monster in me."

"So that was for them?" Lilly asked. Maybe this Jekyll and Hyde dog had just shown her how he could turn from enemy to friend in no time at all.

"Those two are clueless.Their supervisor Adam is a fair man. Has a dog himself I've heard. I also heard he bought this place from his winnings at the racetrack, but I don't know for sure. All I know is what I hear around the yard, because I don't go nowhere else. If Adam had been here he would have put the two of them in their place just now. He would have told them to quit chasing rodents and get back to the cars."

Lilly stared at the dog. "You have a lot of confrontations with thieves?" she asked.

"Some, maybe once a month, maybe twice. Sometimes not for a couple or even three months."

"Sounds like a lonely job. Family?"

"Had a wife. She left me after I came here. Said a junkyard was no fit place for a canine. By that she meant herself. Said she could do better than me and a lot of ugly cars."

"We mice have a life that runs out too quickly for us, so we avoid long courtships and even more divorces. Life is too short for second chances for most of us."

The dog sneezed.

"We're also small enough we can squeeze in and out pretty easily," she noted, not sure where she should take the conversation. A few moments of silence from both was perhaps too much.

"I see. By the way, my name is Boris."

"Thank you, Boris. You saved my life today. I'm Lilly."

"When is your water-thief mate coming with that promised hot dog?"

"He'll be here soon," she responded, with a tone of doubt in her words that she hoped Boris did not detect.

16

Geronimo has responsibility for another near-death of Lilly

Only a short time beforehand, Geronimo had abruptly realized that he had sent Lilly into the salivating mouth of a beastly mongrel! He might throw up, even on an empty stomach, though that would make for too little pain compared to what this dog had done to Lilly. Geronimo could only speculate what the rest of his own and deservedly miserable life should suffer for such a ghastly mistake Ferocious barking sounds had earlier shaken the air enough that the sides of the building vibrated a little, and with it, Geronimo's awareness of how horrible Lilly's end. He could only think of Lilly quivering in her last seconds. Her perils, his own foolish mistakes! He had sent her straight into the merciless jaws of the hungry creature! His ploy to divert the angered men only made his own job of raiding the canteen easier by making it deadly for Lilly.

As Geronimo now cowered beneath the drink machine with hardly a safe place to go, his options for getting outside and to the car diminished. He prepared to spend the rest of his day languishing beneath the humming drink machine and hoping it might fall and crush him to death. A mouse's time on earth was too short already, a year or two at best, and time wasted in creating one's own tragedies, as he had just done, moved the calendar forward even faster. If a mouse could be driven to tears, and that a male mouse, this counted as surely the time for it, Geronimo reasoned to himself, but he had none, only self-hatred, at least for the present. Furthermore, he realized that there was now only one stomach requiring food, his own, so he need not plan for a bag of goodies beyond his own appetite, itself completely absent right now. In a couple more minutes he found some wrinkled grapes and a moldy muffin and deemed this sufficient for the remainder of his day. He certainly would not object if this meal were his last.

With the courage of despair, he carelessly, even recklessly, emerged from his hiding place. Slipping through the crack in the door, he followed the death route he had sent Lilly on, and now stalked next to the building perimeter, still not knowing in his anger if he could bear the sight of a canine that had done such an atrocious deed. He made ready to confront his wife's killer even if it meant suffering the same quick fate of death. No mouse stood any kind of a chance, even an infinitesimally small one, against a muscular and merciless animal. Since death was this dog's deserved end, Geronimo would take comfort in bringing as much pain as possible to the unfeeling mutt.

17

Lilly and the canine Boris confront the hysterical Geronimo

Except for the two men in the building still heard muttering their grievances, Geronimo detected nothing more. Sneaking up to the outside corner of the building, he spotted the mutt flopped on the ground and unmoving. Apparently asleep after his vicious meal,Geronimo still feared his own mousy scent could arouse the slumbering animal until he felt a slight breeze blowing in the opposite direction. If Geronimo had any kind of adequate instrument of death, such as an axe or pick, and the muscle sufficient to wield it, he might possibly end the miserable brute's existence, but he possessed neither. This conundrum counted as another bleak and painful side of mouse existence, that is, the ability to think beyond one's possible means of action. Much as Geronimo loved human automobiles, that attraction, too, came with denial, for a mouse with miniscule body and frame could not drive a car and thus lacked any hope of fulfilling his desire. He even lacked the strength to turn the monstrous navigating circle the humans called a steering wheel.

The furious Geronimo now fumed against his inability to punish the mongrel with the violent death he deserved for his atrocious deed. Geronimo might have returned to the junkyard simply as a concession to reality, for there he could weep for Lilly without anyone else berating his impotent protest, but he delayed, hoping against hope for something ghastly he could inflict on the guilty animal. Truth be told, however, Geronimo had no inkling of how to launch any but the feeblest assault, though such indecision hardly mattered, indeed it mattered not at all, for Geronimo strolled to the other side of the dozing dog only to spot his darling Lilly.

43

Without knowing whether there was any chance that Lilly remained alive or whether she was deceased, he determined to make off with her, dead or alive, while the murdering dog slept. He must remove Lilly and himself from danger before all opportunity was lost! Geronimo placed his small hand in front of her nostrils and to his unmitigated delight and relief felt her warm breath! How she had remained alive, he had no ready surmise. Geronimo must keep the couple safe from a beast quite capable of killing and devouring them both. With his anger returning, however, he failed to remove Lilly from danger before he turned on the mutt as he lost all self-discipline.

"Wake up, scoundrel! You'll pay dearly if you show your teeth," Geronimo charged, knowing such words from a tiny rodent counted as a joke to the dog.

"Geronimo, show some manners," Lilly said, brushing the sleep out of her eyes. "This is Boris," she continued.

In his deep voice and resentful that he must explain anything to a tiny mouse—and one who had now offended him twice in one day—Boris nevertheless made some effort now.

"Before the men could have smashed the life out of the both of you, your mate and I worked a deal," Boris explained.

Geronimo's joy at seeing his beloved Lilly alive and apparently unharmed momentarily overrode any other emotion. But he still distrusted the beast, despite the canine's words, for he had heard what double-crossers dogs could be.

"Where's the food?" Boris demanded.

"What business of yours is the food?" Geronimo asked, perturbed by a beast who now dared to saunter his way into Geronimo's good graces.

"Geronimo, don't. I promised Boris half the food for his help."

Lilly picked up the bag from Geronimo and opened it for Boris. "It isn't much for a creature your size and appetite. You take all of it," she offered, though the mice were hungrier than ever and must do something about the overdue meal they now owed to themselves, for the two men and Adam had left a half hour earlier.

"Let's go back in the building," said Geronimo, now managing to smile a bit and for the first time starting to feel a tinge of sympathy for this hungry beast that he had thought only minutes earlier a murderer. Meanwhile, Lilly reached out her hand for her mate.

18

The first food heist is accomplished

When the pair of mice slithered back through the door crack into the building, Geronimo turned for an embrace that practically took all the air out of Lilly. She did not resist, however, though she felt relieved when the pressure of her husband's arms relaxed.

"I didn't embrace you before because I didn't know the situation and I didn't want to place you in more jeopardy," Geronimo explained. "I mean, the dog might see an opportunity to have two meals in one monstrous bite, and I didn't know what had happened or would. But I didn't mean any rudeness in what I said to him just now. I must say, though, that he needs some training in proper manners. At worst, I figured he was maybe only biding his time until he had us as a meal, so I better not let my guard down, not one bit, in case he tried. I remember the episode at the water puddle too well. But if you think you can trust him, so can I."

"Thank you, Geronimo."

"But how did you cajole him?" he asked.

"I ran straight into him after I came blindly around the side of the building, because I was only thinking of my taunting of the chasers and how laughable the two were. So with hardly time to think of an escape plan since he had me within reach of his chain, I stood frozen and could only imagine his teeth crunching my bones. He was about a foot from my quivering body, though of course standing a foot and a half over me. I only thought of you and my diary. I knew I could not finish the book if dead, so I scrambled to get any words out as fast as I could, trying to persuade him to listen to me. I blurted out that if he refrained from doing me harm, I would give him half of what you scavenged from the canteen. Food proved the key, but I didn't detect that until

"

I mentioned the canteen. When I did, saliva started to drip from his wet jaws like the Falls at Niagara. He knew about the goodies in there, food, I mean. Of course, I figured what you brought out might only serve as a mouse- size meal and could hardly provide a dog-sized meal. Anyway, he consented. If I had offered him money or anything that he couldn't eat, I think he would have eaten me instead."

In three mouse-size trips the two creatures hauled away enough food that even a famished dog would be satisfied this evening. There was a bag of ham slices, in fact three of them, for Geronimo had tied all together to drag out of the building after he found them too heavy for two unaided mice to carry. The rodent cargo carriers discovered tins of beans that they agreed Boris would have no trouble tearing lids off with his monstrous teeth. For their own eat-ing, they found crumbs enough and even a whole single slice of bread. They might have gathered more for their meal, but the hound who had spared the life of a mouse needed a quick and well-deserved dinner.

19

A lavish meal is shared by three new friends

"You'll stay in that coupe here in the yard?" Boris asked as he nodded thanks to Lilly for the feast, with nary a smidgen of anything left.

The two mice looked at one another, not sure who would answer.

"We've stayed in worse," Geronimo told Boris.

"What's your life span?" Lilly asked out of the blue, pushing the subject of cars out of the conversation, though only temporarily.

"Dogs like me live anywhere from ten years to maybe twenty."

"Wow. We mice envy you."

"Everybody wants a little more—most want a lot more—I mean more time than what they can reasonably expect. Even humans," Boris complained. "The life span they've got is the envy of every other animal in the world, except maybe some turtles I heard about. Word is that a significant portion of humans now make it into their nineties," Boris said, almost resentfully. "I hope they're grateful for all that time that others of us don't have."

"Ain't it the truth," Geronimo agreed with a nod, but remained silent afterward, still not quite trusting of Boris, despite what he had said to Lilly earlier. He looked to Lilly, hoping she would carry the conversation.

"Boris, you ever ride in one of those cars out there?" Lilly asked.

"Not one out here. They put them in here when they don't run anymore, or nobody wants or they're just a heap of junk metal. But I did ride in a real car when they brought me out here. It was a truck and I rode in the cab. I saw other dogs in vehicles out on the roads, but I think they ride all the time.

I realized then that being a real domestic dog, I mean a human pet and not a working dog like me, must be a real treat. I mean, riding with your owner like you own the place, puttin' your head out into the wind to see the sights and feel the breeze, and feeling almost the equal of one's owner. Nothing could be better. You want to see an animal that appears carefree and with no gripes and no hang-ups, watch a dog riding in a vehicle with his head out in the wind. I tasted a little bit of that one time. Never forgot it."

"You got options?" Geronimo chimed back into the conversation, and now feeling some regret for his suspicion of Boris.

"I think I must be eleven or twelve years old. Maybe even thirteen or fourteen. Not likely that I' m younger than eleven. The yard in time might want a younger dog, one that's got a little more spunk and fight than me, though I can still frighten thieves plenty when they come."

"You scared me well enough!" Lilly said.

"Me too," Geronimo admitted, and all three shared a laugh, their first.

"Don't exactly know what may happen to me when my working days are terminated," Boris lamented.

The pair of mice looked on without expression.

20

Food heists continue and auto racing unites Geronimo and Boris

In ensuing days, after the men left the yard, and usually close to dusk, the mice routinely plundered for food in the generally well-stocked canteen.Boris's new-found friends habitually found success in that storehouse of goodies. Disappointment reigned when they found too little desired meat in the refrigerator, not ham anyway, or if they couldn't find a pack of hot dogs tucked away in the freezer compartment for the canine. But such was uncommon; ample food was the norm. After the initial days of abundant meals, the mouse pair began to ration one hot dog for Boris per evening meal. Inevitable notice from the stockers, who came every other Thursday, might occur if the animals took too much. In this manner, discipline at mealtime became part of the routine at dusk.

"The men must think they only have a mouse problem, nothing more. What's gone from the trash can they'll probably not notice; the refrigerator they will notice if too much goes too quickly. The men must surmise they ate more than they remembered. If they do notice anything different in the garbage container, they'll maybe set mouse traps, and we can steal the bait for ourselves!" Geronimo asserted.

The two mice normally entered and exited the building through the crack in the south side door and after their first few trips noticed the small garden and an apple tree only a few feet from the building—the tree Lilly came close to crashing into days before. With fall approaching, some of the fruit had vanished, though a couple tomatoes, hardly firm anymore, were easily lifted from failing stalks in the garden.

49

"I haven't eaten this good since I came here ten years ago," Boris said and said again and yet again most every evening.

"I know it isn't quite fair for you, Boris, but we do need to make sure we don't take too much. Otherwise, they'll get suspicious!" Lilly said.

With a smile on his greasy lips, Boris concurred. He had heard the lecture more than once already.

"Tell me about the cars here, in the yard I mean. Are they ever sold?" Geronimo said to his new friend, not wanting to talk only about his food.

"People don't come to buy a whole car, but it can happen. A car may have enough useable parts that someone buys the whole thing, usually to combine with another junker they've got, and if they've got the money for taking one out of here."

The pair of mice settled back in the grass, leaning comfortably against the hound.

"Not one in a hundred of these junkers will ever flop onto a road again. It's the racing cars and their roars at the track that I love, and they never come out of a place like this. If one of them does, then it is money and a restoration genius that are responsible," Boris explained, shifting subjects. "For me drag racing is the draw, if you must know Geronimo, and Lilly maybe told you already. It makes a lot of noise, too much for some, but not for me. This yard at night is like a ghostly cemetery. I need some noise in this place and I get it when the track is in operation at nighttime. At the track, noise is everywhere. When two cars take off, the tires spin out and smoke pours from the wheel wells, but the grandest spectacle though not the loudest is when the car jerks the front end up and off the ground after the green light comes on!"

"So have you ever seen it, Boris?" Lilly asked. "I mean a car doing that."

"No," he said, dropping his head.

21

A dog rides along in a race car

"But I've heard of a dog who has seen plenty racing—even participated."
Geronimo looked skeptical.

"Believe it or not, I hear there's a driver who comes to the track with his dog and that dog rides in the front seat beside the driver! Who wouldn't die to have an owner like him?" Boris offered.

"No! And you're sure of this?" Geronimo asked. "This is no dog lore, is it?"

"Cross my dog heart and hope to die if it isn't true," Boris said. "But mind you, this didn't happen easily. I mean, I think about a year ago an official at the track spotted this dog sitting in a car with the driver right beside him. The official ran out to the car and put up a huge fuss, and everyone thought for sure there would be no race with a dog in that car that day, but it turned out differently."

"So what happened?"

"Well, the car owner was shrewd. He had trained the dog for some months before, so he had his ducks lined up already. He listened to the objections of the officials calmly that afternoon and when he came his turn, he convinced them to allow him to put the dog to the test."

"What test?"

"The car owner had trained the dog to do necessary tasks on command. She is apparently a very smart dog and her owner said later that she was the most trainable dog he had ever seen. In fact, Lottie Dog was so willing to undergo training for that hoped-for experience—I mean riding in the car—that when her master began giving her treats when training went well, she would refuse the treats. Her owner was flummoxed at such behavior, but only for a

51

short while until he figured this meant treats proved no impetus to her, for that impetus to learn and succeed she already possessed. After he figured out her gestures, owner and dog went to work even harder and in a matter of a few more weeks, Lottie could seat herself in her car seat, that being nothing unusual of course, but she could also buckle herself in, just like her master, and as the last thing, she managed to put her crash helmet on without any aid at all. And all of those things she did that afternoon when the track official first objected!"

Geronimo and Lilly were bug-eyed, though Boris was not finished.

22

An escape plan from the yard is revealed by Boris

"Lottie's owner won the race that day, though hardly anybody paid attention to him or to his car or to the victory, because Lottie captured all the attention that afternoon and the next day she was in the newspapers."

"But you've never been to the racetrack yourself or seen this dog?" Lilly asked.

"No," Boris said. "I've never met Lottie, but I do hear the men here at the yard talk about her, so I'll bet they've seen her at the track."

"I see," said Geronimo. "Tell me about this car we're in."

"That car could be pulled off the yard, highly unlikely though, but it could. It probably never will be; as you see, it has a lot of age and rust on it. Not many buyers want a car in that kind of poor condition," Boris explained.

"So no real reason to worry about an eviction coming our way?" Lilly laughed.

"On the other hand, it is a 1948 Ford Coupe, so it has some lookers on occasion, but so far no one has shown interest enough to buy. Meanwhile, for something to occupy me in the long evenings I sometimes try to guess the car that will come out next and if I'd have a chance of getting out of here with it."

"You don't mean leave?" Lilly asked.

"I think about it."

"But it seems quite impossible?" Lilly ventured.

"Maybe possible, but not likely. For it to happen, I'd have to have the details all worked out clearly beforehand."

"But could you pull that off, Boris? Geronimo asked, unconvinced, but willing to listen.

"A ride out of here could hardly succeed because I'm tied during business hours. I could hardly escape in broad daylight, even if I got loose from my chain, I mean without someone noticing me. Nighttime might work, because I am loose then, but no cars go out after hours. And I don't have quite the youthful strength anymore for a jump over the fence, like I once did here in my youth. You see the problem," Boris said.

"Boris, what is that roar we hear?" Geronimo asked, distracted for the moment.

"What day is it?" Boris asked. Geronimo looked to Lilly.

"Thursday," she answered.

"Time?" Boris asked.

Lilly looked around and up in the night sky. "About half after seven," she answered.

"Then those are the cars getting ready. The race starts about eight, but they race in daylight too. I'm told that's a little more exciting—you can see more. But the noise, I mean the music of the racing carries more distance at night—it's almost like I'm right there at the track."

"I see. How far is it from here?" Geronimo asked.

"About ten miles," Boris said. "I heard when the cars take off, the sound of screeching tires and revved up motors up close is deafening," Boris continued, and he smiled broadly.

Geronimo smiled too.

Lilly uttered a good night to Boris and reached for Geronimo's hand as the pair walked back to the 48 Ford coupe.

23

Decisions are made about Boris

"You're in a hurry?" Geronimo asked as they made their way.

"Yes," answered Lilly.

"Why?"

"He has a plan to get out of here," Lilly answered.

"So? I don't think it's possible and he conceded as much. We've made a friend of the animal that almost ate each of us!" Geronimo said, laughing a little, while Lilly showed worry in her face.

"Tomorrow we tell him this will remain home for us—for now," she offered. "Maybe that will put any travel plans of his on hold, at least for a while," she continued. "For us, living in a junked car is not so bad," she concluded.

Geronimo remained silent and simply nodded his agreement.

"Poor creature!" Lilly exclaimed.

"We'll talk with him tomorrow," Geronimo insisted, though his thoughts were elsewhere—on his mate. Maybe Lilly was not the lover of fine things he had presumed or maybe she only wanted Boris to have companions, even if the companions took some getting used to by this dog.

24

Anxiety over the car's possible purchase is considered again

"The car does have a fair number of lookers, but they always seem to move on to look at others. Didn't you ask me that yesterday?" Boris puzzled.

"What color was it?" Geronimo asked, ignoring a little of the irritation he detected in Boris's question.

"Looks like maybe white at one time," Boris said, with better eyes than his weak-eyed mouse friends.

"You know anything about when it came in here?" Lilly asked.

"Listen, I have trouble thinking when I need to eat. Why don't we go up to the building now for our meal?" Boris asked, and his two friends smiled.

Before the two mice went into the building to survey the canteen that evening for tidbits, Lilly went to the apple tree and bit into an apple on the ground. She dragged pieces back to Boris.

The two mice chuckled as they removed peanut bait from the new mouse traps they found in the canteen.

"Such a primitive instrument," Geronimo pronounced. "The stockers will be distressed in the morning for sure, I mean after losing their bait and getting no dead mouse as return on their investment," he laughed.

Meanwhile Lilly managed to get the single hot dog for Boris, and the two mice together collected other food scraps.

"They better keep this space cleaner if they don't want mice getting into the building," Lilly said, and the pair laughed.

Boris thanked them for his hot dog.

"I think I remember now," Boris said, licking his lips with his long hound's tongue. "Two men came in behind the wrecker that brought your car to the yard. There was an older man who didn't seem keen on selling the car to the yard, and a younger one, his son I suspected, who seemed anxious to leave. That was about four years ago, I think."

"You have a strong memory, Boris," Lilly said, impressed.

"Stronger than I wish it at times," he retorted.

25

Boris derides pompous canines and his ex-wife Stratosphere

Mice, though very small and not requiring large amounts of resources, still needed food, some type of shelter, and perhaps some clothing, though the mouse community disagreed over the last item. After their initial introduction to the world, however, mouse flesh grew a thin blanket of sorts. Later, some grown mice did occasionally sport clothing, though the usual preference remained for unclothed body as this presented greater ease of sliding through ever-so-narrow openings and thus gaining entry into houses or churches.

In notable contrast to mice, most canines of the upper classes or those striving to be of that class preferred to present themselves clothed rather than flashing their bare skin, like the untutored barbarians most ruffian-type dogs resembled. While Boris shunned clothing almost of any style or kind, he did not downgrade himself into the ruffian class.

Most everyone had seen a fancy dog or two or three dressed up in some material finery, but Boris mocked such specimens even in dog shows as defectors from their heritage and ultimately weakening themselves so much that after a while these spoiled degenerates registered as good for nothing except for looking spiffy and maybe cuddly. "Work had long ago passed out of their vocabulary and their life," Boris charged. "Heck, I've seen some of these dogs dressed out in more finery than their owners and because of it masters having to do a little moonlighting just to feed and dress these pompous pretenders," Boris continued, with clear and obvious disdain for such vanity. "Such specimens could not defend themselves in the least in any kind of confrontation with man or beast. Even the word weakling is too strong a word for their

59

pathetic state," he added. Boris related how he once had spotted a dog with a gold tooth, which so infuriated him that he told the pair of mice he would have yanked the offending tooth out of the dog's mouth if his master had not kept a suspicious eye on Boris every second.

Evenings of camaraderie amongst the three friends became the habitual practice as Boris regaled his mouse friends with stories that at times made them shudder and other times recoil in fright until he switched to stories with a little humor, and sometimes to wholly humorous yarns. As they listened, the realization that Boris's life had been so eventful the two mice sometimes made the two mice envious, but Boris resented any implication that he had inherited a desirable life just because he had had his share of adventure. Camaraderie soon turned to competition between Geronimo and Boris.

"I've had more than my share of struggles," Boris charged. "You're small enough to do a lot, I mean a lot of things I can't. I'm just too big. You mice can walk out of this place and the wire mesh needn't concern you. It confines me. What it is, is a prison. The wire fence you see around us you can walk back and forth through, but not I. I would like to on occasion, but there's no way. And I can't hide easily in a truck leaving here like you could, either."

"Boris, you haven't been out of here since you came?" Lilly asked.

"Only twice, by going over the fence," he answered, now with a bit of laughter. "My second year here, and still not much faster on my feet than an

overgrown pup, one night after dark I sprinted for about fifty feet and then leaped over the fence, though I grazed my underparts. I had been practicing my sprints the week before. At that time I wasn't intending to run away for good, just hoping for an evening out on the town.

My wife had just left me, I feared for good, so I was a little down, with some appetite for company with my own kind—though not her. Stratosphere—that was her self-designated name—and tells you something about her vanity. In fact, before we married I tried to get her to change that name, but she wouldn't budge. I should have walked right then and there, but I didn't. Too love-struck at the time. Anyway, I tolerated her for about a year and truth be told I resolved to stay with her, though the same could not be said for her. The final straw, with only a year of marriage behind us, came when I was picked up as a stray and brought here to the yard. She told me she couldn't stomach the thought of being married to a junkyard dog. Said it straight to my face, with no care, I don't think, for how much it hurt to hear that kind of remark that cut to the quick from her own over-painted lips. Anyway, I did most everything conceivable to get her back, because I felt something for her, though maybe anger as much as affection. In those days I was young and energetic and so when the men turned me loose in the yard in the afternoon and went home, I would hang out at the fence perimeter to try and see her, because she would stroll by on occasion. I guess she did that when she had no other dog to make miserable."

26

Stratosphere struts her stuff but is humiliated by Boris

Geronimo and Lilly exchanged sympathetic glances as the dog slurped some water. Then Boris continued.

"After more failed attempts for her, I gave up my efforts and quit walking the fence at night, leastways to see her I mean. I had one final encounter with her, which she instigated. I suppose she thought that she would get me to come crawling back if she put on the dog, as the humans say, not that she ever really wanted me back anyway, so I don't know why she engaged in such a silly stunt. That said, I had heard she became all high and mighty in the dog world and more so every day, like those pampered and prissy weaklings I mentioned,the kind that wouldn't and couldn't even pursue a cat up a tree because they're afraid of heights! Sure enough, one evening, about dusk, I was sitting right about here where we're sitting now, minding my own business, and I hear a car drive up and then I hear a door open and close within a few seconds before the car drives away. I figured it might be the first ploy of a thief trying to get into the yard for a steal, so I take some notice. Well, dry my eyes, I said to myself. I saw Stratosphere, though she was hardly recognizable in that getup she wore. She was dressed to the nines in an outfit that must have weighed half her own body weight. That wasn't the most noticeable thing about her, though. She had strong perfume on and if I had been ten paces closer it would have knocked me out and sent me to the ground. I guess she thought her powerful scents too tempting for me and this would entice me to come crawling back to her by leaping over crawling under the fence for her. Then I started to fake gagging noises, like I was throwing up. Pretty soon all the charm comes off of her and she starts using crude language and comparing me to lesser animals, like cats and toads. I could tell she was most infuriated because I would not place myself at her disposal anymore, I mean crawl like some kind of beggar. So as to try to rebuff this act she is putting on, I continue with my throwing up routine and in another minute or so, she stomps off, knowing her stunt had failed. Like no normal dog in this town and scarcely anywhere else in our world, she had a pair of high heels on, whose tapping sound I heard as she stormed away. I still have dreams sometimes where all I hear is that tapping noise her heels made that night."

"Neither of us have any story that will compare to that," Geronimo admitted to Boris as Lilly nodded her agreement.

"Yeah, but truth be told, as bad as Stratosphere treated me, I felt a little remorse afterward, I mean about my gagging and pretended indifference toward her," Boris said.

27

Boris is trapped outside
the yard fence

"You ever see her again?" Lilly asked.

"No. And our world around here is small enough that I should have—if she's to be found. She's probably passed on or maybe she moved away for greener pasture. I think about her on occasion, but grieving over her is long gone for me."

"But you did go out once later, you said?" Lilly asked, hoping to hear more about the incident of jumping the fence.

"Yeah, only last year and right before Adam bought the place, I think. So after my jump over the fence I found myself locked out of the yard after my jump. I beat my head a few times against the fence, wondering how I could have been so stupid as to have no plan for getting back in the yard once out. After everything seemed hopeless, probably around two in the morning, I fell asleep. Next morning when the men came to work they're in a panic when they can't find me because I'm hiding out in the woods next to the perimeter fence. They figured a confrontation with thieves had put me away, but they still couldn't find a dead dog, killed in the performance of duties! They found nothing missing in the office. Meanwhile I was still out in the woods where I could enjoy glimpses of them searching for me. It was a good feeling—I mean to be wanted—even if not for the best reasons.

"Well, of course with the men present, now the gate was open, and so I could have sneaked around and come out into the yard, but I had to create a false scenario that something dreadful had happened to me. So first I found an old wreck to lie in, in a back seat. But I had to sport some realistic scars to

65

authenticate my faked injuries, for when they finally did find me. So I took some barbed wire and cut myself in a few places and smeared my face. After that I made some muffled barks to attract their notice, but no one came running! I looked up at the sun and figured that it must be lunch time, and so I knew they might not hear me if they're eating lunch in the canteen at the back of the building.

"Meanwhile, I needed more realism, and I came up with it. That is, the blood from my self-inflicted wounds needed to be mostly dry and have the look of being on me a while before they finally saw me, so I remained in the car seat while they ate their lunch. Sure enough, in a half hour or so, for whatever reason, I hear them calling my name again, so I managed to feign a cry of distress loud enough for them to hear and they all came running. They treated me with some real kindness and respect at that time, but little afterward. Even gave me some popcorn one of them had brought from home for his own paltry meal. I actually started to figure the experience might provoke additional treats from them. Instead, after a few more days they insisted I could go back to work for them on the yard, and the tasty tidbits that had been mine for a few days stopped almost as soon as they had started. Adam bought this place just weeks afterward, and soon he showed real concern for me. The two men already working here were good enough with the wrecks that Adam kept them on, but they never befriended me like Adam.

"When the men later told Adam about the incident, he took me to a veterinarian to assess my wounds from the 'accident.' Since my physical maladies were superficial and more importantly, self-inflicted, this was one time I was glad that I could not communicate with humans. Anyway, I stayed at the clinic overnight for what they call observation and even had a nice evening meal and dreamed later of Stratosphere eating at the table across from me. The next day when Adam came to take me back to the yard he brought a few extra treats and this bed roll. After that, I made no further attempt to get out of the yard again."

"Quite the story, Boris," Lilly commented.

Geronimo smiled, but said nothing. He noticed a tingle in his stomach not felt before.

<h1 style="text-align:center">28</h1>

Geronimo and Boris square off

After his story, Boris smuggled assumed that a tiny mouse living in a tiny world could not possess any stories comparable to his own. However, when Boris mistakenly said as much out loud, Geronimo took Boris on, jealousy as much as anything being the catalyst.

"Truth is, Boris, we wee animals are the toughest of all animals because we have had to think quickly to compensate for our vulnerable small size. You monstrous animals just stand there and, because of your bigness, a smaller animal may simply turn tail and run from you without any fight at all. We mice have not been handed a physical means for intimidating enemies. We muster strength to stand our ground and fight, or else we run as rapidly as our tiny legs permit, but of course when the latter, we give the false impression of being cowards. But we are not. We must make split-second decisions about our best course of action. I dare say birds of prey leave you dogs alone, but mice are the favorite dish of these winged wretches who regard us as the primary staple of their diet. One on one, we stand not a chance against them, so we have to outthink them, because we aren't big."

Boris offered a perfunctory apology to his friend for doubting that a mouse had stories of danger like his own.

"Apology accepted," Geronimo said. "Your misapprehension is understandable. But as I explained, we mice must make ourselves the equal of many an aggressor who is at least a hundred times our size and weight and usually much more. That means, Boris, that we have to think, to think smart, and think beyond the limitations of our tiny frame, if we are to have a chance of living in the world at all."

"I'm listening," said Boris, though still with a doubting demeanor couched in his tone and on his face.

"Well then, my canine friend, I'll tell you how we in the mice world go after the malicious giant predators coming at us. I don't know the circumstances of your wedding to Stratosphere, but of ours I dare say it evidences how our most important life occasions are riddled and badgered by larger animals," Geronimo asserted, still smarting over Boris's earlier proclamations.

Lilly regretted such harsh words coming from Geronimo, and feared what might happen next, for he was not above exaggerating to embellish a tale. Lilly cleared her throat just a little and Geronimo glanced in her direction.

"Lilly had her heart set on a church wedding," Geronimo began, ignoring Lilly's signal. "We were all ready to make our residence in the church house. Trouble was, to put on a mouse wedding in the sanctuary of the church, even at a late hour, might provoke suspicious humans to run some kind of interference. So we decided to move the wedding outside, though this of course presented the problem of winged predators who controlled the sky and a lot of trees. A mouse by himself or with company in the big outdoors invites alert and even sleepy predators, so I contemplated what to do and came up with a plan that all of our wedding party and all of our kinfolk to this day still talk about—Lilly included."

Lilly grimaced as Geronimo caught his second wind. Boris yawned to show his boredom. Lilly seemed equally annoyed at both.

Geronimo, irritated by Boris's demeanor, hastened to speed up his story in case Boris fell asleep, but no words came.

"Cat got your tongue?" Boris interjected, as he opened his eyes, with Lilly looking askance at the canine's tone. She nodded to Geronimo to continue, but Geronimo began to cough.

"Lilly, perhaps . . . . you can tell the story," Geronimo managed to say before he resumed his cough.

Lilly no sooner picked up the story than Geronimo's cough accelerated. A few minutes later, with his cough under better control, Geronimo insisted that he was okay. This was his usual response to any such inquiry about himself, though as soon as he tried to start his telling of the story again, Lilly thought she saw a wink from her husband. Lilly cast an eye at Geronimo, and might have taken the occasion to take aside and rebuke Geronimo, for Lilly now suspected her husband might be faking out of irritation with Boris. For now she would simply try to ignore him.

"He might just need rest," Lilly offered, prepared to dismiss Geronimo's antics.

"Listen, I didn't mean to insult Geronimo's story," Boris said.

Lilly wasn't sure if there was a morsel of genuineness in such an apology and paused for a few seconds. Geronimo kept his eyes closed, coughing occasionally for empty effect, she reasoned.

29

Boris reveals his loneliness to Lilly

"I want to hear more about life here on the yard and after Stratosphere. So what about your years here?" Lilly said to Boris.

"Mostly, I imagine what might have been."

"What might have been?" Lilly asked.

"If Stratosphere and I had made it."

"I see. You still care for her?"

"No. I mean maybe. Some days I imagine life with her, and that after all our troubles." The canine laughed a little, with a glance toward Geronimo, who looked out cold.

"No other friendships, romantic ones I mean?" Lilly asked.

"No. A junkyard dog is low on the totem pole, maybe the lowest of the low, especially when it comes to female friendships. He's thought as useful to fight intruders, but not to make a home or raise a family. Mostly his kind end up loners if they aren't already. If he takes a bullet from a thief and dies, it's no real loss to his owners; they just get another dog. But a dog doing what I do has to have some expertise, some brains for this job or he'll be dead sooner than he figured. To manage a lookout and keep thieves at bay is not so easy. Stratosphere certainly never understood all it took to do this job."

"No other romantic friendships after her?" Lilly asked again.

"Oh, sorry. Not really. I've noticed some females over the years, on the other side of the fence of course, but close enough for me to get a good look, and them at me.I wouldn't have minded striking up a conversation with them, but I knew the minute they realized my occupation they would shove off. Plus, the humiliation of that kind of rejection is just too much for me, even after just one encounter, I mean with Stratosphere. I try not to think about it anymore."

"Sorry," said Lilly. She wanted to pick her pen up and put a few of Boris's words for her diary, but feared he might object.

"Don't be. Sometimes it helps to talk about one's disappointments."

"So, never anyone else?" She scrubbed the idea of writing and would simply listen and remember for her diary.

"Not of the romantic kind. And almost no friendships until Geronimo and you came along."

"Boris, that's terrible," Lilly responded with sadness in her voice and tears in her eyes.

Boris dropped his head and said nothing.

"Do any of the men ever come out to play catch?" she continued.

"Adam. He knows I'm not the vicious type and he keeps me on here because he realizes I've got fortitude enough to protect this place so he can relax when he goes home. He knows too that though I can put any thieves to flight, he need not fear so much as a scratch from me.But he's busy with the wrecks and sales and customers and all; I can't really expect him to devote himself to a hound who needs company.

"Anyone ever consider getting you a companion?"

"A while back. I think it was the time they suspected I might be dead, I mean until they found me. Then the old days resumed. Beyond that, nothing that I know."

Lilly stared at the canine.

"You have to get back up on the horse even if the horse has thrown you a country mile," Boris said. "You and Geronimo have done that? I mean coming here—certainly not the easiest adjustment for a couple who were once church mice, living in near paradise, as you described it to me, I mean. As for me, it's my fault I didn't try more times to get out of here." Boris dropped his head and Lilly pulled out *I Climbed a Mountain* to try out on her canine friend.After Lilly briefly introduced the story, Boris readied himself to listen, this time without any feigned boredom, as Lilly gave a glance toward the sleeping Geronimo.

After Lilly read some humorous passages from the book, she had to pause for Boris to control his laughter enough that she could continue. What would have ordinarily been only a half hour to tell the beginning of the story of Ephraim Mouse, turned into a full hour of amusement for the two of them. Meanwhile, Geronimo remained fixed on the ground, even when Boris shook with uproars sufficient to virtually vibrate the ground. And there was no wonder, for Lilly's commentary on the story proved nearly as entertaining to Boris as the story itself, with Boris insisting each time on hearing the next episode, until Lilly said they must stop.

"That must be for another time," Lilly said, anxious to get Geronimo up.[3]

"I'm sorry, Lilly, for my earlier antics. Please tell Geronimo when he wakes."

----

3. For interested readers, something of the concluding part of the story of Ephraim Mouse goes this way. When the now old mouse made his way back down the mountain, he discovered that his spouse had died some decades in the past and that the members of his family currently living were his great-great-grandchildren and were well-nigh worthless and, worst of all, were astonishingly disrespectful toward their venerated ancestor. However, with some feigned pretense of respect for their long-gone ancient relative, one of them suggested the mountain climber write a book about his adventure. At first resistant, he changed his mind when the young relative offered the old man free clothing and room and board and anything else he might need if the old man would write the book. This the old gentleman could not resist because of his love of recounting his lifetime of adventure. He told his inquiring relatives that he had rather move his fingers than force more work on his tired and worn-out legs. However, the adventure having been so far in the man's past, at least the uphill climb, he had forgotten the most basic information about his journey and so instead, and unknown to his provider, he began to write about the topsy-turvy and chaotic nature of the household of his relatives in which he now found himself forced to pay for his keep until he finished the book. The old gentleman penned tens of passages in the bulky book that were libelous to his caretaker family, and the publisher withdrew his offer to publish the work unless the said passages were removed. The author was adamant that nothing be removed from his pages, and hearing of the incident, six other publishers lined up to take on the book just as the author had written it, and without any editorial redactions. By the time the book finally came out, with a new publisher, and savvy and expert enough to earn Ephraim Mouse stupendous royalties and himself a very tidy sum, the book in no time at all graced the domicile of every literate mouse household.

30

The health of Geronimo takes a downward turn

For Lilly to get food out of the canteen by herself the next evening, without Geronimo's aid, proved more than difficult—it proved impossible after a quarter hour of solo effort. Lilly had covered Geronimo up with a light sheet from the car and signaled to Boris that the two of them would have some dinner soon, but she later found herself mistaken, for there were the expected leftovers in the trash, though much less than usual, and hardly any dog fare Lilly could reach. Frustrated, she slipped back outside where she presented hardly more than and end piece of bread and scarcely any meat for the hungry Boris.

"This is not good," Boris lamented as he gobbled the modest offerings from Lilly.

"What do we do, Boris?"

"Those big doors on the other side have a button to push that sends the door up. If I could get inside, I could push it, but I can't get in the building without that door up. But if you can find a piece of twine from inside and rig it to the button and then bring the string to me through the door crack, I think I can manipulate the button and open the door." Boris was as mistaken as Lilly in her earlier efforts to get more food from the canteen, for Boris's exertion on the string was too much for the feeble string which snapped every time Boris pulled.

When Lilly insisted they make one final effort after multiple defeats, by some mysterious maneuverings the door went up, and without either of their efforts. Boris immediately trotted into the building and just as soon headed for the canteen. Lilly scampered behind him and on arriving at the food, pointed out to Boris where the various foods were stored. So excited was Boris to enjoy such a feast of foods, that Lilly offered no reminder of excessive food intake that might create suspicion the next time the men returned. Boris informed Lilly that this was only the third time he had ever been inside the building. The former occasions he had been escorted in by the men of the yard.

After eating was over and Lilly anxious to attend to Geronimo, Boris was insistent to spend just a few minutes more in the building, until for unknown reason the door went back down. Boris's surmise was that the door was on some kind of timer for up and down when it detected activity in the building. Nevertheless, when the door came down, the delight of being inside the building vanished, as Boris could find no way to send the door back up to enable him to get out. Boris finally went to sleep in the building that night, quite unplanned and not enjoyed. Meanwhile, in the Ford Lilly tried to keep Geronimo's chills under control by piling on pieces of car upholstery, some darkened by blood stains but other pieces in near perfect condition.

Lilly had had no success in explaining to Geronimo that she had mistakenly interpreted his condition the evening before, because he lay unconscious. His cough and his sleep were not fabrications by him simply to annoy Boris, as she had suspected the prior evening, for only a few minutes after crawling back into the car, he had lost consciousness, with nary a word spoken. When the coverings placed on him from the car proved insufficient, Lilly placed herself close enough to feel his shaking chills.

31

Boris scurries to avoid detection

At the first sound of the men arriving the next morning Boris felt panic-stricken when he heard Adam calling out for him. In a stroke of absolute luck, after Adam entered the building he strode toward the rear. This proved just the break Boris required for coming out of hiding and darting swiftly out of the building and toward his stake, ready to congratulate himself on his quick maneuver. Adam who habitually gave Boris at least half a hot dog before he chained him up outside for the day, patted his head as usual and headed for the canteen. Eventually, he found the desired item, came out and tossed it to Boris, the canine now relieved his misadventures of the night were apparently unsuspected.

"How did you sleep?" Lilly asked a quarter hour later, knowing that Boris was aching to relate how he found his way out of the building without discovery that morning.

Instead he asked after Geronimo.

"He's not awake," Lilly admitted.

"I see," Boris said.

"When was the last time he spoke?"

"He babbled a bit yesterday, maybe a couple minutes, no more," she answered.

"But he still drinks water?"

"Yes."

"And when you feed him, does he ever open his eyes?"

"Only one time."

"Does he chew when he eats?"

"Very little. I mush his food so he can mostly just swallow it with water."

"Does he ever choke on his food or the water?"

"Rarely, but Boris, am I talking to a doctor?" Lilly said quizzically. Boris grimaced.

"My father at one time worked as a doctor, on dogs I mean. Never taught me any more about medicine after my brother and I made him ashamed of us when we failed at the dog track. In fact, he virtually never spoke to me or my brother after our stunt of not winning races, by losing them by a country mile. That's when I turned to comedy routines. Laughter eased some of the pain, I guess, but it was definitely more to my liking than running races that I could never win. Around that time, too, though maybe a little later, I started to get interested in car racing. But let's get back to Geronimo. You ever know a mouse to have tick fever?"

"Yes. That's what killed Geronimo's siblings some time ago, I mean a few weeks ago. Only he and his brother Maverick survived. Neither of them ever showed any signs of it, while the others nearly dropped like flies."

"Maybe he has shown nothing till now, if I can speak so frankly, Lilly. I mean this may be the fever that got his siblings. I might suggest if you have communication with the surviving brother, you let him know about this. "

"Of course, but I'm hoping in another day or two his fever breaks again," she offered.

Lilly had to beg off from Boris to return to Geronimo and finally did after ten more minutes of conversation over health and indeed death with the canine, who might have been a dog physician Lilly learned, save for his father.

"Hungry now?" she asked her mate.

Geronimo shook his head, but he did open his eyes.

"What would you like? I have a little cheese, some pieces of apple, a couple peanuts, and a piece of apple muffin." She hoped something sounded appetizing to him.

He stared at her for about a minute without words and his eyes, though weakly open, exuded a droopy and sleepy look, as if he could not focus his eyes. Lilly reached to take his hand, and then her heart sank when she squeezed a second time as his hand went limp in hers. His head fell backward onto his pillow and eyes shut.

32

Geronimo evidences serious sickness

Minutes later he sat up, but he looked none the better as he glanced quizzically at his surroundings.

"Where are we?"

Thank goodness, he could talk. Lilly paused before she answered, not knowing what answer might help him the most, but grateful that he had spoken.

"I was afraid the dog had got you," he continued.

Lilly started to tear up a little, but dared not let Geronimo see.

Her thoughts were suddenly broken by a groan from Geronimo and she reached for her small container of water for him. His eyes did not open, but his mouth did and he sucked in enough of the wetness to resume his sleepy state.

She went across the car seat and brought out *I Climbed a Mountain*, opened the book and looked at Geronimo. Maybe he had an appetite for something else.

"I am going to read a bit," she said. "For you, but also for me," she added. Without any further fanfare she started to read from the beginning, but her words stopped after a couple tries. Lilly decided she might instead expound a passage from the book, though that failed too. She would simply talk to him and hope he heard something.

"We have passed through valleys before, though maybe none like this. But we can still train our heads and our eyes to look up to something greater than what we mortal mice in hidden and dark spaces normally see, if we see at all with our weak eyes."

Geronimo made no motions nor emitted any sounds as she spoke, and Lilly tried again a minute later. This time the reading of *I Climbed a Mountain* proved medicine enough, and she forgot their troubles for a short while.

33

Separation of friends
haunts the future

The next morning began like any other day. That is, after Lilly attended to Geronimo she paid her usual visit to Boris, with no new news to report on Geronimo's condition. By afternoon, however, as she sat by Geronimo something noticeably different filled the air and Lilly set to worry after she heard barking from Boris. Although he had barked frantically before, she could not imagine his agitation now, except to suspect that something threatening had transpired and that the two mice should stay put. Straining to get a glimpse,she could see that Boris sat fixed on the ground like a lawn figure dog, with his gaze toward Lilly's direction while an older gentleman with his walking cane stood in the driveway with the building at his back, obviously waiting for something. He looked at the dog and smiled as he reached over to pat Boris on the head.

"Shall we take a look at her?" he said to the men who came out of the building and now walked in a direction toward the 1948 Ford Coupe. Lilly could make out a few of the men's words as they came closer. After another minute Boris launched into barking again, painfully louder than ever, and finally Lilly understood. She hurriedly began to pack.

After another minute of frenzied getting together the few mouse belongings and trying to get out of the coupe quickly and undetected, Lilly concluded such effort fruitless and decided instead to hide their belongings behind the back seat. A few odds and ends she stuffed into her pockets. With only a few yards or so between them and the advancing party of men, she and Geronimo must hide themselves, so she pulled Geronimo quickly from the rear seat to

79

the trunk of the car. She had no sooner found and slipped through a crevice for the two of them when Geronimo's eyes suddenly opened.

"We have to maintain silence," she whispered, as she heard the approaching human voices and crunched leaves suffering human feet. Geronimo only nodded his head, but said nothing and his eyes closed again. Lilly dropped her head and tears unleashed as she put two protecting arms around her mate.

Boris continued to bark incessantly, while Lilly could now make out most of the talk. The men were discussing how much work the car required, and the buyer expressed regret that he had ever brought the car to the yard. Soon their conversation shifted and jostling began over the price for the coupe until an agreeable sum was settled upon. Everyone shook hands and the men walked back to the building, occasionally laughing among themselves.

A flatbed truck would pull the coupe from surrounding overgrown greenery, while the frantic barking of a dog fearing loss of his friends escalated. The driver squeezed the truck close to the coupe in only a few minutes, but required a half hour to ratchet the dilapidated coupe from strained limbs of surrounding vegetation. For her part Lilly felt hidden safely enough in the trunk with Geronimo, though she expressed no relief even at seeing Geronimo's eyes open again. A chainsaw came out from behind the truck cab and severed the final resisting limbs still grasping the car body. With the truck cables tugging with an unpleasant scraping noise, the salvaged wreck emerged from the undergrowth, and in a few more minutes the old coupe was fastened down sufficiently for transport. Lilly's tears poured into her lap as the truck left the tangled mess of vegetation. The purchaser came closer to the building, oblivious of the consequences of the deal just transacted. The crusty automobile he now owned again. A younger man carrying an oxygen tank got out of their car and shook hands with the older gentlemen and with Adam.

The incessant barking resumed, as the new owners walked down to the driveway, waiting for the heap of weathered metal and sun-bleached upholstery to come to them. Boris now barked with the ferocity of a mad dog, and the two buyers moved further away from the canine. Adam spoke to the dog who then relented from barking and whimpered loudly instead. Adam rubbed the dog's head and side, feeling the raging heart of the animal pulsating through his thick skin. Lilly knew Boris could not be mollified. When the truck driver started to leave the yard for good, the new owners of the old coupe following in their car, Boris erupted again, now with bone-chilling urgency. The ferocious sound could have stalled or even stopped in his tracks the vilest thief. Boris leaped upward and marshalled enough adrenalin strength to pull the stake and the chain from the ground, the same kind of strength he had boasted to Geronimo about weeks before at the water hole. With his new freedom, though only for a brief minute, Boris jumped again and this time onto the back of the truck, the chain and anchor tagging along around his neck.

The two yard workers shouted reprimands to a dog whose job it was to stop thieves and not upset paying patrons, while Adam came closer to Boris again and moved to take him down from the trailer, which did. The dog fell silent except for his whimpers but did not resist Adam's firm hands. The new owners prepared to leave again, after shaking hands all around. Lilly wished she had not seen or heard any of the altercation.

When Adam took Boris down from the trailer, the animal responded with cries so despondent that Lilly, inside the dilapidated coupe, cringed as she wept—even after she could no longer see her canine friend. The forsaken dog, in his desperation to not lose his friends, now gave up his failed effort and resumed whimpering as Adam continued to hold the weighty mongrel in his arms. Lilly and Geronimo would presumably spend their night in the heap, but at another location and not with Boris, who now had the junkyard to himself again.

34

Lilly assumes the mantle of leadership

Virtually all responsibilities for the two mice now fell to Lilly. Even if Geronimo in the future could manage a full or nearly full recovery, fever had stolen health that might not return. She would need to make allowances for a physically weaker husband now and regretted the distance separating them from a friend. Boris's cries echoed in her head and interrupted her sleep in the night.

"I climbed a mountain," she said out loud, and the familiar words awoke Geronimo out of his slumber.

"Wonderful," Geronimo said, but the awakening appeared to expend all energy and his head dipped backward as he slipped into fevered unconsciousness again.

The night made sleep no easier for Lilly, even while hidden within a familiar automobile. Lilly might have Geronimo back, she hoped, at least a little. She needed him to console the her over what had happened that afternoon, for the bond between Geronimo and Boris had taken some time to solidify, and just as it did, the two friends encountered this separation. Now she regretted any impatience she had shown, and rather obvious to the two of them she knew, when the two car lovers had conversed over the subject Lilly cared little about. Suddenly her tears erupted as she wanted to console the two of them, for Boris would have to endure his evening without his friend and amongst a ghastly yard of dead automobiles again. There was no race at the track tonight for Boris's ears either. Though Geronimo had Lilly, in his state at the moment he was hardly aware of his surroundings or that Lilly would now be his protector over the coming days.

Lilly got up and crawled through the interior of the old coupe down to the trailer bed and then dropped down again onto one of the tires and finally to the concrete floor. The interior of the building looked extraordinarily well kept, much cleaner than the interior of the building at the junk yard. The structure appeared a working shop, with dozens of tools placed in organized fashion on walls and side tables. Hanging on one wall were three pictures of the 48 Ford Coupe in better days. A light layer of sawdust covered the floor, for oil and grease, Lilly suspected. The sawdust, which must have been fresh, emitted a woodsy and pleasant scent in the garage. These things, however, were not in Lilly's interest tonight, and she headed toward a small refrigerator, hoping it would provide at least food enough for one night. She did not suffer disappointment, finding lunch meats and morsels of cheese and raisins and other such tidbits. Lilly was hungry enough that she started to eat right away even before climbing back up to the truck bed and the car. As she settled herself near Geronimo, she realized that they would need to find other housing before the new 48 Ford owners detected the presence of mice within their new purchase from the junkyard. The burden of the thought sent her to sleep quickly now, even as memories of Boris intervened. Geronimo slept fitfully.

35

Reconnaissance is done
on a Tudor house

The next morning, with Geronimo resting rather nicely, despite eating little, Lilly made her first venture in the dangerous outside. Two hawks spotted Lilly as she backed up against the metal garage to survey dangers and opportunities. One puddle of water about twenty feet from the south side of the building would prove too risky for a drink. A hundred feet away and across the driveway sat the residence, a Tudor house, or rather, almost a mansion. Despite the view, she hurriedly retreated to the garage.

That morning came without human visitors and in the afternoon Lilly began to plan her night trip to the residence while Geronimo slept most of the day. When he opened his eyes near dusk, Lilly told him what she had seen thus far and details of her plan for an after-dark venture. The two held hands for a while and Lilly added more details of what had transpired at the junk yard and with Boris the day before.

"Stratosphere," Geronimo managed to say, but he said nothing more, while his eyes stayed open with apparent expectation of a story—so he got just that from Lilly.

"Well, Boris told me this story more than once, so I have it down." Lilly noted that a weak smile came onto Geronimo's face. "He said almost every dog parent expects that their offspring could compete at the dog track, and some parents are so keen on it that they start to train their children for racing when weaned, with the expectation that in time they'll have a winner at the track that could make their parents big money. Boris's parents proved no dif-

85

ferent, so they touted the same unrealistic dream to their offspring. Boris said the average dog might as well bark at the moon than spend his days training for a race they could never hope to win.It's thoroughly unrealistic, he said, that a dog as slow on foot as him and his brother would make it to a level like that, just like the human kids we hear about thinking they might make it to the professional level of some uppity sport.Anyway, Boris and his brother had enough sense even as youngsters to not waste their youth training for a race they knew they could never win. Indeed, he said that after running their first race they decided on another option with which to build a reputation. Boris said that he and his brother made it their goal to run so slowly in their races that the scheduling officials frequently had to postpone the next race because Boris and his brother were always finishing later than anyone expected and of course delaying the next race!

"But then something happened, Boris told me. People started to come to the track just to see two of the slowest dogs in the county trailing every other dog. Oddly enough the track owners didn't seem to mind, as long as ticket purchases didn't suffer."

However, when his parents heard of him and his brother's unusual fame at the track, they were so embarrassed they forced the two to quit the track altogether. His brother meanwhile ran away from home and never returned, presumably due to his inability to overcome his embarrassment about his track reputation, though he and Boris had in the beginning colluded together on their plan. However, from that experience, Boris ventured into comedy routines and believed that the track experience taught him he could make people laugh and that he really could entertain people, especially if he didn't take himself too seriously, as his brother apparently had. Moreover, he suspected his comedy routines had nudged Stratosphere to take interest in him, except then he lost his job at one comedy club through a misunderstanding with the crowd about one of his jokes and then he was blackballed. Afterward he had to settle for being a junk yard dog, and Stratosphere lost interest in him then, he said."

36

Entrance is gained to the Tudor house

With hungry predators scavenging for food after dark, night hours become more dangerous for small animals. Lilly had figured her time for a one-way trek to the prospective dwelling should take no more than ninety seconds, but as soon as she had the building at her back, and two or three seconds had elapsed, she heard unfriendly wing flutters and then the sound of her furry hide scratched deeply enough to bring blood. Once lifted into the air, Lilly's only hope depended on being dropped in flight by the bird and that at very low altitude, though such luck rarely materialized, tonight it did, and the blood-spattered mouse found herself only mildly bruised after a drop from a few vertical feet.

She nevertheless regained her composure and her courage and resumed her sprint and soon safely sat down, hidden behind a bush amongst the many planted alongside the Tudor house. She then paused to survey the outside structure and her opportunities for getting at least a look inside and maybe even a visit. She must search for the safest point of entry, always away from any space congested with human traffic, while doorway cracks offered places of opportunity for squeezing inside without crushing one's own insides. The first door examined was so tightly shut that no light from inside escaped. In another minute Lilly had moved halfway around the house searching for another entry, but stopped on finding a sliding glass door providing wide visibility into the house. The curtains had not been drawn for the night.

Lilly positioned herself at one side of the door and studied the inviting view. There were no people, none seeable at least, though perhaps in other rooms at the moment. Better yet, no visible cats roamed about. From her vantage point Lilly could easily see one side of a gigantic table in a dining room. The kitchen surely lay closely adjacent, though Lilly could not see it even when she slithered to the other side of the sliding doors. Presently two adults came and sat down at the table, the man carefully tucking in the woman's chair before he sat and then leaning his cane against the wall behind him. Almost before he seated himself, the woman fell out of her chair. Without fanfare her husband helped her back up again into her chair, and Lilly wondered if this was a habitual occurrence. She also immediately recognized the man as the purchaser of the 48 Ford Coupe. And then Lilly saw what was a sure sign of a well-supplied house: a female cook in occupational clothing served both adults. There must be plentiful food scraps in waste bins in the kitchen of this Tudor house, Lilly told herself.

Chatter between the couple accompanied their meal, and Lilly understood most of the dinner conversation even at some distance. On one occasion the gentleman even leaned over to kiss the lady's cheek and then resumed his meal, while he shared a story about the vehicle he had owned some years earlier, but had now repurchased for their son. Lilly even heard Boris's name mentioned, but could not discern any details. Lilly now dared to allow herself hope that this might be their new home. She would make it even more comfortable than the church house. She knew, too, that for all of Geronimo's love of automobiles, he preferred not to live in one, even a 48 Ford, but in a house. To Lilly, this one would do just fine.

37

Preparations for safety are made

The next morning Lilly insisted to Geronimo that they visit Boris as soon as possible after securing a domicile inside the house—if they did. Geronimo offered no argument on the matter to Lilly, though both mice knew that, marvelous though the house seemed, neither of them had yet been inside. The matter of this residence would remain unsettled until they could gain entry and that not before Geronimo had adequate strength for a dangerous night-time venture. The entire planned reconnaissance event required probably an hour, Lilly reasoned.

Meanwhile, Lilly's eyes had earlier noticed the small roll of barbed wire wound on a plastic spool and hanging from the wall in the immaculate shop. She immediately went to work to fashion a cylinder-shaped basket, providing a mouse body on the inside protection and not restricting the use of the hands.

Geronimo suddenly took notice.

"Who said I married you only for beauty!" Geronimo blurted out, on seeing that the awkward and clumsy-looking contraption might work. Lilly had forced into circle shapes a half dozen rounds of barbed wire for protection for a mouse lodged within the confining suit.

"When we get to the Tudor, we'll pull it off," Lilly advised, before she noticed the fatigue on Geronimo's face again. He made no objection to Lilly's insistence on a rest and soon fell asleep while Lilly quietly removed herself from his side and checked her list for the night journey.

When nightfall came the next day, and after their being delayed a day by Geronimo's bout of fatigue, Lilly dragged the ludicrous-looking contraptions out of the garage. Barbs scratched and drew some flowing blood from Lilly before she finished fitting Geronimo in his protective suit with less trouble than putting on her own. The-suited up duo exited hastily from the building and attracted no enemies from the air this time. With his extra day of rest, Geronimo felt well enough to cast colorful derisions on the unseen usual assailants, suggesting the birds in hiding of lily-livered cowardice.Getting out of such contraptions after their arrival at the Tudor house without more blood-letting took as much time as putting the contraption on, but the two mice in a few exhausting minutes walked free of their protective suits that Lilly, with a little help from Geronimo, now hid behind a shrub.

Wasting no time, Lilly ran a quick trip around the house perimeter, but all the outside house doors, four of them, so squeezed any door frame that there was not even space enough for a slender mouse to slip through.

38

A catapult comes to the rescue for obtaining valuable information

"What now?" Lilly asked, with some despondency on her face. She need not have worried, as Geronimo turned to Lilly with a smile she had not seen in some days.

"The catapult launch?" he offered.

"We can't shoot out a window!" Lilly objected, having seen the simple weapon, really a customized slingshot, in use by Geronimo on other occasions.

"No. We make attracting noise by hitting the windows. All who are in the house will come to investigate. Fetch a limb and we'll fashion our weapon."

With further details agreed upon, and noticing Geronimo's enthusiasm for his project, Lilly's apprehensions faded. The two mice spotted a perfect candidate shrub for the needed limb, though it took a quarter hour to separate it from the bush and another quarter hour to rest their fatigued mouths.

"We'll need some pebbles, about the size of the tip of a human's little finger, no bigger. Three people in the house, did you say?" Geronimo asked.

"Three," she affirmed.

"With the size of this house, there may be more. When the pebble hits the bay window we'll see. We'll just stay out of sight and count people and hope none are already in bed. We may have a chance to see any dogs or cats, too."

Geronimo had insisted on making this venture with her, despite his lingering fatigue. Though glad she had yielded to his request, she knew that at any time he might simply roll over on the ground.

His pebble rifled from the rubber band slingshot and pinged the glass hard. Safely hidden, Lilly and Geronimo now waited. After two minutes no one had yet appeared at the large bay window.

"We need more bang," Geronimo decided, and this time he shot two pebbles from his weapon. A woman came to the window, looking puzzled, but not alarmed.

"We'll try another, too," Geronimo said.

The third effort hit the window even harder and the woman returned and now looking worried.She soon stepped away and reappeared with a flashlight. Behind her came the older couple.

"The younger woman is the cook. I saw her last night," Lilly said.

"I'll not send another noisemaker. That might create enough panic that they end up calling the police," Geronimo explained.

"So what now?" Lilly inquired.

"We'll stay put for a little while yet. It's best to be sure about our people count."

In another half hour the first-floor lights went off, though second-floor lights remained on.

"The elderly couple probably sleeps on the first floor, and the younger woman as a live-in housekeeper and cook, as you expected, must have her bedroom upstairs," Geronimo surmised.

"But we can't get in for a better look! I'm no better off than two nights ago," Lilly lamented.

"Don't think so?" asked Geronimo, who had managed to do some of his own reconnaissance around the house perimeter.

"Did we miss a door?" she asked.

"Not down here, but on the second floor. I'll bet there's an outside door up there to get in the house."

Geronimo soon depleted his remaining energies for the evening and dropped to the ground but now tried to stay awake while Lilly found her way to the second floor. She uncovered an outside stairwell virtually hidden by overgrown holly shrubbery and climbing rose trellises too, but she managed to squeeze through the door frame gap though pointed holly leaves and rose thorns as obstinate as barbed wire itself pricked her sensitive flesh. On the other side of the door was another bedroom, and a human asleep. She slipped quietly out of the room, as she caught sight of an oxygen tank beside the bed.

If the outside of the house had awed Lilly, the inside did more. The spaciousness of the bedrooms—she counted four—were beyond anything Lilly Mouse had ever seen in both size and splendor, but she needed to hurry and not engage in fantasies. She scampered about searching for any place that might accommodate a pair of untroublesome mice. Fortunately, she glimpsed several possibilities, enough to assuage any further worry.

Geronimo was asleep on the ground and almost impossible to rouse. After a quarter hour of exhausting effort without success, Lilly finally located a puddle of water and cupped her hands to deliver the wet stuff to Geronimo's sleepy face. It worked. His stamina, however, would be tested only minutes later.

39

Return to the '48 Ford coupe proves difficult and dangerous

They had ventured back toward the garage when a winged predator descended and threatened what had been an evening of successes. The suit of barbed wire proved hardly invincible, however, and the hopeful hawk shoved his razor-like claws into Geronimo's maze of wire in an attempt to seize the flesh within. The insistent bird might as well have flown into a prison cell, for the protecting cage turned into a physical and mental nightmare for the stunned hawk, who soon found his beak nearly immobile in the wire jungle. Unable to lift his prey or scarcely even himself off the ground, the stunned bird tried to poke at the eyes of Geronimo as a way to defy the small creature. Lilly now came around the back side of the bird to harass the predator fowl.

"Roll!" Lilly shouted to Geronimo, herself now taking charge of the counterassault. The beak of the offending animal remained bound in the barbed wire, while the two mice continued to incapacitate their victim. To add insult to injury for the stymied fowl, Geronimo managed to produce one of his magical rubber bands and wrapped it around the trapped beak. Given another rubber band, Lilly succeeded in wrapping the bird's feet together. The angry bird by now had ceased to desire a meal of mice or a meal at all and instead flung his head in every direction in a vain attempt to be free of the odd contraption and the menacing animals.

Though the stymied predator did manage to escape more degrading humiliation after another minute of resistance against his attackers, the decorated bird in hours to come would suffer jokes and laughter from an audience of his own kind. With his hasty and unglamorous escape, the two mice speculated that the offended bird had retreated to a nearby tree, or perhaps sought out other territory as a place of sanctuary. There he might hide his shame and consequent lost authority as a previous warrior of nature.

40

A visit to Boris becomes a serious matter

After nearly a week in their Tudor living facility, the two mice started to bask in the homey atmosphere felt in every corner of the house and began to call the place home. Sure enough, the live-in housekeeper/cook did have her living space on the second floor, only two rooms removed from a spacious corner closet that Lilly and Geronimo had chosen for entryway to a safer and more secluded residence in a comfortable and private attic. One day, after a few days of cautious observations, Lilly nearly panicked, fearing that perhaps the woman had actually spotted the female mouse, if only for a split second.

"There was no screaming, no indication that she found my presence terribly upsetting or anything of the sort, assuming that she did see me," Lilly told Geronimo.

"But now we need to talk about Boris," Geronimo began. "I found a map of this village two nights ago and I traced the way to the junkyard and Boris. It's further than we could travel on our own. Is there any way the four people here could aid us, Lilly? I mean for a trip to Boris. I know you have been watching them, like hawks watch us! I mean is there anything to know for a trip away from here?"

"The maid has her own car. She shops twice a week, mostly for groceries and toiletries.Those trips are on Tuesday and Friday. She leaves to shop right after she has given the couple and herself breakfast; that's about nine o'clock. She stores her grocery bags in a storage area in the kitchen, and so I know the store name and found the location on your map. Judging from the map, her store looks only about a mile from the junk yard. So, I propose this: if we can

95

ride along somehow, I mean with her, we can get started toward the yard and Boris. When to do it? Today is Saturday. Why don't we rest tomorrow and Monday.Meanwhile, I will get us ready for our trip on Tuesday."

With this much of her plan presented, Lilly made lunch and afterward joined Geronimo, now in bed again.

As Geronimo noticed, Lilly had observed the routine and movements of all four persons in the house, almost down to minutiae. She knew the location of food resources, though she never intruded into storage cabinets or anything of that sort, for the garbage bin provided food enough to recover for two mice with miniscule diets compared to weightier humans. Many a time over past days—though always at nighttime and after all lights were out—Lilly had gone into the garbage container with something hopeful in mind, only to come out with something unexpected. Of rich food there was, and thankfully so, not much, as a mouse was as susceptible as most every other creature to adding more body weight than advisable, though Geronimo's appetite these days was most always less on any current day than the day before.

41

The oddities called humans are subjects of thought for two mice

More absorbing to Lilly than the food and even the beautiful Tudor house was the couple living in the house. The previous church house had provided the rodents only tangential viewings of humans, and never much of a lens on how members of a family related with one another. She and Geronimo had guessed the couple in the Tudor in their mid-sixties, an impossible achievement of longevity for even the longest-lived mouse to contemplate. In *I Climbed a Mountain*, the reader understood after a while that the hero of the story was given allegorically long years of life to climb and descend a mountain that a normal mouse lifetime never came even close to achieving.

As disclosed already, hardly any reality relentlessly badgered a mouse more than his brooding awareness of a very short life span compared to other animal populations. Furthermore, many adult mice so lamented this incontrovertible fact that some underwent counseling at some point to manage their anxiety. Eternity, it seemed, pounded in some tiny mouse hearts, while their physics kept mice pinned to earth, no matter how much they incessantly craved more years that early death denied them.

No mouse, it would seem to follow, with this kind of burden to bear, could live a life given to frivolity, yet some did, as likewise some humans did. Lilly and Geronimo had had exposure enough to humans to readily observe the unstated commitment to a frivolity that seemed the guiding light for some, however likely to result in unnecessary pain and suffering. These kind of humans seemed incapable of turning in another direction or making any advancement at all in their mode of being. Geronimo and Lilly had for long wanted more up-close observations of the remarkable species of humans, at both upper and lower levels of being. Living in the Tudor house now gave them some more opportunity for the former. The men at the yard had given them some opportunity to observe the latter.

Reading seemed a favorite pastime of the human couple in the Tudor house, starting at breakfast and not ending until the two, already in bed and preparing for sleep, finished the day with more reading, though usually no more than ten or fifteen minutes before sleep. About a half hour after the couple retired, the live-in domestic, having finished in the kitchen, retired to her bedroom and read for most of an hour, unless a favorite television show competed. Sometimes Lilly and Geronimo heard her laughs and figured that such was the reason for keeping her door shut. Whenever she had a visit from the couple's son from two bedrooms away, her employers had asked that she keep her door open, as they greatly enjoyed hearing the chatter of two people who had once been very close, and still remained friends after Charles's health began to fail. The son very seldom went out on his own anymore.The trip with his father to repurchase the '48 Ford had been his first outing in almost a month. Meanwhile, slurred speech in the early evenings from downstairs sometimes prompted Lilly to suspect, though hardly with adequate evidence, that the wife and mother might be an alcoholic.

The couple almost never came upstairs during the day and even less in the evening. If the daytime weather was nice and not too cold, in the daytime the couple walked around the edge of the estate, and as the Tudor yard and perimeter gardens proved quite large, traversing around the space twice constituted their limit.Sometimes, however, they walked both mornings and afternoons. Almost inevitably such a walk meant a nap or at least a sitting rest afterward.

Reader that she insisted upon being, Lilly made visitations to the couple's library when safety was assured, that is, when everyone else, including Geronimo and the maid, slept. Lilly observed that Charles almost never went downstairs and certainly never in the evenings.

42

The mice begin their journey to visit Boris

Wanting to prevent the maid from suspecting stowaways, the two mice waited three full minutes by Lilly's count before they unhooked from the car chassis and crawled out. The ride had taken six minutes and sprayed a colossal amount of water over the two stowaways. Now upright again, the pair scurried across the parking lot, dragging their wire protection over wet asphalt.

"At best, three quarters of a mile, but probably a mile," Lilly relayed to Geronimo. "We'll stop to rest as often as you need," she continued.

"How about we leave our cages, hiding them in the shrubbery over there," and he pointed. "I mean until we return?" Geronimo proposed. Lilly would not hear of it.

For the first hour of walking, the pair encountered no immediate dangers, though they did spot one hawk surveying these mice walking within the absurd-looking cages. Perhaps cautious predators had heard the cautionary tale of one of their species suffering and being humiliated with his mouth closed by a rubber band. Both mice laughed as they recounted the event to one another.

"I wonder if he wrote home about his dilemma!" Geronimo jeered.

"Of course!" said Lilly. "He would have to write, because he can't talk easily with his beak recovering," she added. Geronimo had to stop walking for a bit to control his laughter. The three cracked ribs, though healed, or so he thought, still pained him a bit.

Geronimo's own stories, despite the competition from Boris in days past, were now the main entertainment for Lilly, even if she had heard most of them

101

before. After a particularly hilarious story, Lilly asked if the Mouse Brigade had taught him story-telling along with combat survival techniques.

"They taught me both," Geronimo answered, before he pointed out a puddle of water for a drink and both crept up to the watering hole for the needed moisture. Minutes later they headed for some shade to take a rest, though the sun in October was not oppressive. Their resting spot proved too comfortable, however, as Geronimo fell asleep under the leaves of the small tree.

Any fatigue from walking paled in comparison to the anxious anticipation of seeing an old friend again. Both mice knew Boris must expect that his friends would make their way to him eventually.

43

A surprise at the junkyard overwhelms Geronimo and Lilly for a while

The-ever-so slight coolness of the October afternoon breeze prompted a bit more vigor in their steps after the rest. Without a single serious interruption of their journey by predators, and despite three more watchful hawks perched in lookout trees, Geronimo and Lilly arrived at the junk yard an hour after the men usually went home. Now nearly dark, the two mice slipped easily once again through the woven wire fence, but neither saw nor heard their canine friend. Almost immediately, the two mice panicked, simply because Boris could detect every smell and hear every sound issuing from the yard, but there was no barking now, not even a whimper. The two rushed to Boris's area. The space was bare, with only an empty water dish and a food dish—also empty. The two mice stared at one another, neither daring to surmise anything, for in Boris's absence there were few comforting explanations to render realistic hope. In the desire to refrain from comparing painful inferences, the two walked around the perimeter of the building in opposite directions, hoping for some positive hint of the dog's whereabouts or existence.

When Geronimo spotted a chunk of grass reddened with what might be blood, he called Lilly. Neither said anything as the two looked at the ground and then looked at each other blankly.

"No way to tell exactly where this came from," Geronimo said.

"No. Why don't we go inside and look around?" Lilly offered.

The two made their way through the entryway of the bent door, but nothing seen or heard or smelled provided any clue about Boris.

"The only clues are his empty dishes and the red stuff on the ground. If something happened to him, I mean something like getting really sick, the containers would have gone with him and if he is gone for good, then the men would have acquired another dog to protect the yard. There's no replacement canine here. It's a good sign, Geronimo."

"Makes sense. On the other hand the men may have got so upset with him when he objected to us leaving, that they got impatient with him . . . . "

"They had the normal aggravations humans have with dogs, but they would never let him go and furthermore, Adam would not have let that happen. They at him for sure, but that only happened when they couldn't quieten his barking, like the day we left."

"Why don't we see if there is any food in the trash for us?" Geronimo tried to smile as he spoke.

44

Two mice are at a loss over the whereabouts of Boris

When the yard men arrived the next morning, Geronimo and Lilly noticed that they made no calls for a dog who may have hid himself or may have made successful escape from the yard. Everything seemed normal as the two men went about their routines, while the mice worked fervently to position themselves within earshot for any talk of Boris. The morning, however, produced frustration with no forthcoming clues and left the mice exasperated. After that the afternoon dragged on, with still nothing that gave any clue about Boris. When the men were just about to go home and the two mice had largely given up any expectation of news from them about Boris, Lilly heard one of them mention his name, but nothing more. The two mice scurried furtively closer and waited with desperation for something else, however little. And then it came—something neither could hardly bear to hear.

One of the men said he was bringing a new dog the next day and they would try him out. They could not risk another night with the yard unguarded, he said to the other. Meanwhile, Lilly's heart almost stopped and she wanted to step forward in haste, ready to question the men, leaving fear and better judgement behind for the moment, but she dared not. After all, her human language ability was not all that strong.

The night would be well-nigh sleepless for both of them, and they decided it best to be gone the next morning before the men came to the junkyard again, as the mere sight of them a second time might be too upsetting for the pair.

45

Two mice plan for a way to the racetrack

"We need to get out of here now." Lilly said the next morning, as she readied their two suits of barbed wire from outside the fence. "I don't want to see Boris's replacement," she added. "Let's go."

"You've got the map," Geronimo reminded Lilly as he followed her lead.

She scarcely unfolded it enough for a look.

"Let me take it," he offered and Lilly handed it over.

"I have an idea," he said.

"About the map?"

"No. I know who might know something about Boris."

"Who?" she asked.

"Lottie."

Lilly paused. "But we don't know Lottie."

"But Boris did."

"But we don't know where to find her."

"Yes we do."

"We do?"

"Yes. She rides in a racer and the town went all berserk the first time she did it, remember?"

"So we find Lottie at the drag strip! When? " she asked.

"Friday nights. Leastways that's what Boris told us."

"How will we get there?" As soon as she asked, Lilly felt even more than silly. After all, Geronimo's catapult had worked for their reconnaissance mission at the Tudor house. Surely he could find a racetrack and provide a way to get there. They turned their backs to the junkyard and began walking.

Ten minutes later Geronimo remembered that Boris had said the trek from the yard to the track was ten miles. He kept quiet for a minute and then told Lilly. No mouse, even one with fabricated wings, could travel such a distance before he died of fatigue or simply crashed, as a wing broke off and the machine descended full throttle to the ground. Geronimo prefaced his words with caution before he gave her the news. "Lilly, we have a mountain in front of us," he said and then he told her about the ten miles. She said nothing at first, but then put her head in her hands and began sobbing quietly. Geronimo stretched out as best he could in his barbed wire suit, until he twitched and forced himself up. Lilly assumed the barbs had pricked his skin.

"Help me get this thing off," he ordered.

"We can't take it off; you'll be a meal for a predator in no time," Lilly asserted.

"Take it off," he said again. With the sternness in his voice, Lilly would not argue.

"You do have a plan?" she asked.

"Not fully, not yet," he said, as Lilly eased him out of his protective suit. "Lilly, somebody once told me, and I cannot remember who, that when my own strength fails me, I should look up. By the way, we'll need your suit, too; turn around and I'll get if off, and then maybe my idea will make sense."

Lilly almost looked annoyed. "Talk to me," she said.

"I think we can make it, I mean to the track, even if it is so far away we could never walk it, not even come close," he explained.

"So what do we do?" Lilly asked.

"We need a car," he explained.

"And how . . . ," Lilly began.

"We need one to stop, but they can't know they're stopping for us, and they wouldn't understand anyway."

"Geronimo, you've lost me."

"Time to sit up," he said. "We'll get a car to stop and use the occasion to slip into the car, out of sight, of course."

"And we're chauffeured to the racetrack?" Lilly asked in an almost mocking tone, convinced that Geronimo had scrubbed the line between reality and dreaming. Not until Geronimo explained again did Lilly finally start to nod her agreement about a mass of details that Geronimo enumerated. She had the easier task in Geronimo's elaborate plan, she told herself, as after an hour of still more details, she walked back up the road to spot any candidate cars that might carry the mice to the track instead of them having ten miles to walk.

46

Two mice execute their plan for a ride to the racetrack

Over the past half hour Lilly had counted thirteen cars that had passed her by, but none had sported a racetrack sticker on their bumpers or anywhere else. Positioned about three hundred feet or so from Geronimo, her job consisted of signaling to him for any car approaching him from her direction and headed toward the track that brandished a racetrack sticker. The mice had surmised that a passing automobile going in the direction of the track and with such a sticker was perhaps a likely candidate for their hoped-for ride to the track.

Mouse eyesight, as mentioned numerous times already, was terribly weak, so a handwave or something on that order was simply too hard for Geronimo to see, and with such small bodies mice could hardly make out each other at such a distance. But after Geronimo's earlier exhibitions of what his vaunted rubber bands could do, Lilly suggested her own remedy: a viable slingshot that sent small stones at near ground level up the road that Geronimo could see by their bouncing motion. Coming at him as moving objects, they would indicate the approaching car was designated by Lilly as a candidate to halt. Meanwhile, Geronimo would ready himself for the candidate car and driver. Of course Lilly's job would not yet be finished, for she must immediately run as fast as she possibly could to Geronimo to prepare to get inside the stopped car with him, while the driver changed his flat tire.

To force a car into stopping would prove relatively easy since Geronimo had hit on another use, in fact the final use, for the protective suits. The barbs laid down in the road would force the car to stop; he would rubber band together the two suits with the barbs positioned to accomplish the greatest penetration of the tire, forcing the driver to stop and change his suddenly flat tire! The mice would now have their opportunity, for once the car was saddled with a sudden flat tire and Lilly had arrived at the car from her lookout point up the road, and as the driver got out to change his tire, the two mice would without any fanfare choose an inconspicuous place to hide in the car, which allowed them to see the racetrack entrance and sign when it eventually came into view. Precisely upon seeing the track entrance, the two mice would then make every attempt to show themselves, with mouse screeches included. Of course they would expect the driver to exhibit all the hysteria humans are known for on finding mice in their automobile.

Most importantly, only when the car had proceeded about ten miles and come close to the racetrack, would the mice show themselves to the driver and/or passengers, and of course in the certain fright of discovering such varmints in his car, he would stop as quickly as he could and attempt to send the two packing. Naturally, this would mean that he would open a door or doors to chase the guilty pair out of his vehicle. The two mice would avoid any confrontation—their only desire was to be let out of the car with the driver happy to accommodate. Thanking the driver for the lift would certainly be inappropriate, however fluent Geronimo was with the human language.

47

The afternoon is devoted to rest after an unorthodox trip to the track

The task of changing his flat tire the driver accomplished without difficulty, while the two mice hiding beneath the front seat had communicated by hand signals and uttered not a single word. A passenger remained in the front seat, though the driver had insisted she get out of the vehicle with him, though she had refused. The demeanor of the mice, exhausted though each one was, exuded happiness for once, for the past hours had sent them into such a spiral that at an earlier point they had almost given up the attempt to get to the track. They now chastised themselves for the thought.

As the man resumed driving with the passenger the mice assumed as his wife, the mice were content to simply wait for their opportunity. The couple in the front seat exchanged no words of genial conversation, which made Lilly think the two might have just had a fight, but there was hardly any way of knowing. Humans Lilly almost always found interesting, but now she paid for her inattention to Geronimo, as she looked at him only to see a sleeping mouse!

Her first thought was to pinch him, but he did not so much as even flinch, so she pinched harder, but still nothing. By now two or three minutes had elapsed and at least a couple of miles on the road were behind them. Suddenly Lilly realized she had to care for two things, a sleepy mate and a stringent watch for an entryway sign to the racetrack—and that by herself. She began doing everything she could think of to rouse Geronimo, starting with putting her fingers into his mouth until she realized it might make him gag, with the noise arousing the attention of the couple too soon. Lilly then tried pulling on his mouse hair, on both arms, but still with no success. When every ploy she could imagine, short of slapping her mate with a swift hand, failed, she decided that as soon as the sign to the track appeared, she would pinch his nostrils and his mouth closed, and that would surely wake him. If his sudden gasping aroused the attention of the couple in the front seat, that was of no matter, because the two mice must exit from the car at that point.

Lilly now knew, more than even three minutes ago, that everything in their plan to get to the racetrack depended on her, with their next item being simply to get out of a stopped car, after she showed herself to the humans sitting in the front seat. She therefore inched upward on the back of the front passenger seat for a better view of the roadside, and just at that moment, and exactly then, she saw the entrance sign for the racetrack not a tenth of a mile ahead. She paused for only a second to judge if the driver was in fact slowing for the entrance driveway, and when he showed no sign of that, Lilly jumped down onto the lap of the female, who, true to the reputation of women in the presence of small rodents, screamed. The scream was so loud that even Lilly panicked for a brief moment, but in her hysteria still managed to remove herself from the woman's lap by a jump onto the automobile dash, directly in front of the driver, who now slammed on his brakes, pulled over to the side of the road, and immediately jumped out of the car, leaving his door open as he looked for something, anything, to swat the squatter mouse with. The woman, too, jumped out of the car, still screaming, though not as loudly as before.

Despite the rapidity of events, and trying to avoid any blows from the humans, Lilly had not forgotten Geronimo, but she still had to work her way into the back seat to retrieve him. Lilly could now see that he had not moved out of his slumber despite all the commotion. Realizing that the possibility of death for her or Geronimo or both escalated for every second this standoff continued, Lilly went forward a few mouse paces and stood on her hind feet and flouted her tail at the woman, who promptly fell backward into the shrubs in the side ditch. This gave Lilly the perfect opportunity to pull Geronimo from the car. The female mouse quickly slung her mate onto her back and out of the car.Meanwhile, the car driver was in the side ditch trying to awaken the woman.

Neither party ever saw the other again. Meanwhile, Lilly awakened Geronimo and told him what had happened. She would record virtually all of it in the diary that night. Before the sun was at its zenith, the two mice sought a resting place under the protection of two bushes with limbs and clinging leaves hanging low enough to provide a canopy. So as to relieve their latest episode of stress a little more, Geronimo took out *I Climbed a Mountain* and proceeded to read one of his favorite passages of courtroom drama from the popular book. While neither one rolled in laughter from the story as they usually did—their hope to locate Lottie and good news about Boris still uncertain—they nevertheless could not maintain too somber a face when Geronimo read from the old man's account of his court misadventures years with his relatives after his heroic deed of mountain climbing.[4]

---

4. The mountain climber, who had expected to be treated at least humanely, if not honorifically by his younger kinsmen, discovered one day that these unscrupulous characters had pilfered through his earnings from his famous book, and had also forged a reverse mortgage, making themselves the recipients of monies due their famous relation. When the infuriated old man demanded a correction of such vice, the relatives balked and even dared to laugh in his face. Unmoved as the mountain he had climbed years earlier, however, he enlisted the aid of a lawyer and took his conniving relations to court to demand his money. His offending relations, all eleven of them, were so brazen as to stuff and swell their pockets with some of the stolen money, showing no sign of remorse or indeed any feeling at all until the judge and jury ruled that the mountain climber was due his money and all eleven would be committed to imprisonment until the last penny was paid to their relative. The reprobate eleven—their nickname amongst the village people—laughed at the decision and prepared to leave the courtroom without more hindrance to their day, until the elderly mountain climber, not prepared to suffer this kind of humiliating debacle in public as he habitually did at home in private, stood up and, after consulting with the judge, proposed to battle each of the eleven in a game of arm wrestling and should any of the eleven win their contest with the old man, that thieving relation could keep their stolen money. At such a proposal the reprobate eleven fell into a bedlam of panic over the mere thought of such a contest and half of them dropped to their knees in a posture of deference to the court and their ancestor, but when not a single one submitted to the proposed contest, all went to prison.

48

Two mice have a fruitful afternoon at the drag strip

The racetrack seemed the draw for everyone on a Friday night, just as Boris had said, for the place looked as though young and old, firm and in-firm, babies and grandparents, and everyone else had come. And with all the excitement of engines roaring and tires screeching and the front ends of cars jumping into the air unnecessary for a couple seconds on takeoff, no one bothered with any mice, except for an occasional child who found the sight of the little creatures every bit as eye-catching and interesting as the monstrous and deafening automobiles. The two mice soon found an area underneath the bleachers, where dropped popcorn and other pieces of snacks provided a welcome treat.

Between the bleachers and the race cars and drivers and mechanics and an assortment of other people lay the track itself. To get to cars and drivers meant crossing the strip of asphalt, the very ground where the monstrous machines took off and propelled down the track at incredible speeds. The mere thought of close proximity to such dangers almost crippled the two tiny mice for a few minutes, until they noticed how easily people managed to maneuver safely through the area of danger.

The pair hardly attracted any attention at all except from some children, as race fans.were used to seeing field mice scurrying about from cornfields that surrounded the racetrack on two sides. Geronimo remarked to Lilly that the track layout with its neighboring fields was really quite lovely, though Lilly knew Geronimo remained enticed more by the cars and the track and ear-piercing engine roars than by any docile and quiet corn field, however beautiful. Lilly remained focused on finding Lottie and could not be distracted.

Although there were quite a few racing cars for their weak mouse eyes to survey, if Boris's remembered story about Lottie was accurate, they should have no difficulty spotting a dog inside one of the cars, or easier yet, a dog at all and one positioned in a car! The pair spent the next minutes squinting at cars, but no car showed any sign of canine presence. Meanwhile, two upcoming racers inched their way to the starting line from their separate lanes for what now looked like the first race of the afternoon. Each car crept up to the starting line like lions poised to attack prey and then settled into a few seconds of what was called "peeling rubber," car jargon for warming the tires up by breaking traction causing clouds of billowing smoke to fill the air. Then the cars would return behind the starting line again and wait for the green light. The whole show proved thrilling for the mice to watch, though Geronimo more so than Lilly, and he hurried to warn her to cover her ears, and only in the nick of time, as the cars took off. True to form, the front end of both cars came off the track a good eight inches or so, just as Boris had described. For Geronimo the race was disappointingly short, being over in only a matter of seconds. Though the track measured a quarter mile, it took the well-crafted engines hardly any time to transport the monster machines to the finish.

Almost as soon as the first race finished, Lilly noticed the second pair of cars beginning to approach the starting line. Suddenly, both mice at once squealed as loud as a mouse's lungs permitted. They had spotted a dog in the passenger seat!

"That has to be Lottie!" Geronimo shouted.

"Yes, she looks just like Boris described her." No sooner were these words spoken than the driver and his canine passenger began to pull helmets over their heads.

"This is their race!" Geronimo said. "We may have to wait until they're finished to speak to her," he added.

"No," said Lilly with urgency in her voice. "Their car could crash on the track and we'd never get to her. Let's go!"

Geronimo followed Lilly, who now maneuvered herself through the maze of tools and people without being stepped on, intentionally or accidentally, and finally made her way to the car containing Lottie. Both mice now managed to grip the front passenger tire and claw their way up the round rubber. Leaping from the tire onto the car body, they came around to the windshield and then back to the open window of the dog's seat.

"Boris. We can't find Boris! Can you help? We think you're Lottie."

The dog pulled around to see who was talking, and though at first appearing frightened at the small rodents, quickly regained her composure.

"I know where he is. I don't have time for more now—get in and hurry!" the canine commanded. "Put these ear plugs in your ears."

Both mice did as instructed and Lottie immediately tossed them a small belt rope and told them to fasten themselves to the seat.

"Put your back up against the seat and cover your ears," she instructed. "Everything will be all right, just hang on."

Sure enough, the driver inched up to the starting line and then let the monstrous motor heat up the tires with a roar and smoke such as they had seen earlier. In another two minutes both cars sat behind the starting line waiting for the green light. The lion sat ready to pounce. Lottie turned back to them again.

"No worries," she said and smiled.

Only seconds after the dog turned to the front again, the green light came on, and both cars erupted with an explosion of roars and tire screams and the habitual front end jumping skyward. Geronimo had a splendid view of the helmeted driver in action and his skillful shifting of gears. In no time at all, the car was at the end of the track, Lottie's owner winning easily by a quarter car length. Geronimo, practically in happy tears from the whole experience, however brief, immediately turned to Lilly, who smiled but anxiously waited for more details about Boris.

49

Mysteries are revealed

"Boris is recuperating," Lottie offered.

"From what?" Geronimo blurted out.

"He's alive?" Lilly asked.

"Another dog might have died. He took two bullets from thieves in the yard. He's convalescing now. He won't police the car yard again after this, and he's goanna need some time to get his strength back for much of anything. He speaks of you both often," Lottie said.

"You've seen him?" Geronimo asked.

"He's at my house," Lottie offered. "Adam and Francine's place."

With the driver's helmet pulled off her head, she came into plain view for the tiny mice.

"Adam's wife, Francine," Lottie explained.

Francine shook her tied up hair loose as she looked away.

Geronimo looked on in disbelief while tears poured from Lilly's tiny eyes.

"Something wrong?" Lottie asked.

"No, nothing is wrong," the two mice said to Lottie almost in unison, and both wreathed with smiles now.

Lottie asked how two miniscule mice got to know the canine and thus began the tale of their own misadventures, most all shared with Lottie.

When Geronimo told the story of their fatiguing journey from the church house to the yard and to the Tudor house—and the unbelievable plan the two mice had conceived to get to the track only a few hours earlier, the canine insisted the two mice be taken to their destination.

"You must visit Boris soon," Lottie said to Geronimo and Lilly on parting. "He will be expecting you," she added.

119

50

Lilly and Geronimo visit Boris

The visit to see Boris proved safe and was made more enjoyable by the platter of dainty morsels provided for guests, but the pair of mice could not manage to hide their overriding shock at the sight of Boris's wounds from his altercation with thieves.

"The whole thing happened three days after the '48 Ford left with both of you," Boris began. "There were two of them. I must confess that if I had given more attention beforehand, they might not have gotten through the gate at all, but I didn't notice them before they had cut three locks and were already coming in," he added.

"Before that?" Lilly asked.

Boris hung his head a little. "I was over in the area where your old coupe had been," he responded.

"I see," Lilly added, without more comment.

"You had a confrontation with them right away, I mean, when they first saw you?" Geronimo asked.

"My fault again. I should have stayed hidden and anticipated their likely plan a bit more before I made my move, because only one of them was armed. I should have taken more notice before I threw myself at both of them."

Geronimo looked puzzled, as well as exhausted.

"The unarmed thief drove their truck inside the opened gate and then got out and walked over to his accomplice, who was pointing to one of the wrecks, I guess the one they planned to steal. I held back a little, but then jumped them from behind. I did knock both of the scoundrels down and could have handled one easily enough, but the other with the gun used it on me, almost

hitting his partner on his first shot. Instead it hit me. And then he fired another shot at me, the second bullet I took."

"It's a miracle you're alive at all, Boris," Lilly said, with tears in her eyes too large for her host not to notice.

"That it is, Lilly. Fortunately, neither bullet hit vital organs, but my strength is only very slowly coming back. No more yard work for me."

"We heard," Lilly offered.

"Maybe I could go back to doing comedy routines," Boris suggested and the two mice smiled.

"How about the thieves?" Geronimo asked.

"Turned tail and ran after the sounds of their gunfire brought the police!! Heck, they skedaddled before the police got to the yard," Boris answered, laughing a little as he said the words.

"Not funny then, I guess?" said Lilly.

"Oh no, of course not. They did run though, just like cowards," Boris answered.

"But how about you? What was your condition then?" Geronimo asked.

"I had lost blood but I could move, though ever so slowly. I had seen a couple wrecks come in that afternoon that had not been stripped yet, so I figured one might still have a battery that would enable me to sound the car horn.

So I pulled myself over to the closest one, but its battery was already gone. I went about thirty more feet for the other one, and found reward for my effort. I knew by hitting the horn I could make some noise that might bring someone to help, so I just lay on the horn and waited. That was when the police came and found me. They phoned a veterinarian on call, who came to his surgery around midnight. Without that kind of help, I would have been a dead dog," Boris concluded.

The two mice smiled at their canine friend.

"Well, enough about me. I want to hear about you. First, the story about your wedding, and the trick and traps you laid for the predators, since the ceremony was going to be outside. By the way, I apologize for my antics that evening; I mean when you tried to tell the story."

"I have no story comparable to yours, Boris," Geronimo confessed, though he said it with a smile.

51

Tragedy strikes

As October marched toward colder November, the couple spent almost all their days in the Tudor house, and only rarely went out as Geronimo's condition turned into a steady decline of already weak health. He experienced increasing fatigue coupled with a recurring fever, which ultimately exhausted him. Despite Lilly's careful nursing, his remaining strength slowly ebbed away. Though Lilly saw his death coming, when it arrived she plunged into grief, and worse, a grief born of some resentment. She had to concede, like every other mouse who had pondered the mouse predicament, that life was extraordinarily short for these creatures and there seemed no remedy for a death coming so soon after birth. Even old soldiers in time must give up the fight for more days, a realization in Geronimo's last day in the Tudor house that he admitted to Lilly. So, increasingly fatigued and badgered with the fever that incessantly recurred, exhaustion steadily took the last bit of energy and he finally expired.

Maverick his brother had traveled in haste and with hope to see his dying brother, but he missed the end of Geronimo's life by an hour. The same day Lilly and Maverick would wait until the humans were all in bed before they removed the body from the Tudor house for burial to a pre-selected spot by Lilly, just off the boundary of the estate property. Each said a few words over the deceased before the wails of both of the tiny animals pierced the dark nighttime. Lilly had not only herself to console, but Maverick too, while she worked at patching up his cuts and bruises from combatant predators encountered on his journey. The two meanwhile provided stories about Geronimo that the other did not know, and both found some humor in them, despite the occasion.

Before he became bed-ridden, Geronimo had been lifted for a final visit to see Boris, but instructed that he must give no hint of the forthcoming celebration of Boris's heroism. Boris was his old self during the visitation, but the dog never sufficiently recovered from his wounds, though he was taken for regular visits to the veterinarian. Twice it appeared Boris might be improving, but the morning after the ceremony for Boris at the racetrack, Lottie began to bark incessantly for Adam and Francine, both in the back yard refurbishing a weathered doghouse for Boris. On first sight the retired junkyard dog appeared comfortably asleep in his bed, until the couple determined Boris no longer breathing.

The ceremony of the prior day honoring Boris at the racetrack had proved too much for the canine, who had been worn down by his years of heartache, mixed in, of course, with a colorful life on many an occasion. Even Stratosphere got wind of the event and made an appearance, though in disguise. Before the races that afternoon, a track official had presented a medallion, which he hung around Boris's neck, with the words "For extraordinary courage in the line of duty." The hound made no speech, only a simple thank you and even turned down an invitation to ride in the car with Lottie and Francine, insistent

that it was thrill enough simply to be at the track. To hear all the motor noise up close and not from ten miles away was delightful to Boris as tears of happiness ran down his face.

The canine would be buried in Adam's backyard. The two men at the yard had been noticeably shaken at the news, aware that Boris had heroically resisted the assault of thieves and was hardly the impotent dog they had hurled insults at some weeks earlier. In consultation with one another, the two men along with owner Adam decided to close the yard for a day and hung a wreath on the locked front gate.

Notice of Boris's death got out to the wider community of dogs—presumably through Lottie. The news was greeted with the greatest grief from his most recent friends, the animals who knew him best, particularly Lilly, though also Lottie and even Stratosphere. Anyone who knew the canine in life rightly figured that Boris's toughness had been for the most part contrived, though requisite for the business of guarding automobiles when barriers proved inconsequential to unscrupulous thieves. True, on two separate occasions, but early on in that relationship, Boris's two mouse friends had nearly perished at the sight of his razored teeth and threatening, salivating mouth. At the time, the big animal and the tiny ones had been hostile strangers to one another and had not yet established their later strong friendship.

Stratosphere herself, whereabouts or existence previously unknown, managed a visit to the gravesite under cover of darkness, and neighboring dogs later reported that her wails were so loud and protracted that other dogs close by, who had at first responded to a visiting canine on their turf with two minutes of retaliatory barking, became silent out of respect for her obvious and sincere grief.

52

A new life is made and an old book found in the Tudor house library

On learning of Boris's death while still in mourning over Geronimo, Lilly searched for comfort that eluded her, but she found some solace when she returned to her book, and particularly as she read and reread the entries from her beloved diary. Her book, mostly written from incidents recorded in the diary, mused on the painful beginning of having to leave the church house. She placed every remembered incident into her pages, both the pleasurable and painful ones, and of course events involving Boris and stories he told.

Detailed work on her story drew her back to fond and also sad memories of their last days at the church house, though very soon other matters intervened in her new life.Less than a month after marriage to brother-in-law and now husband Maverick Mouse, Lilly gave birth to a litter of little ones. Aside from giving needed attention to a new husband and being occupied with first-time mothering, she often persisted with work on her book until late in the evenings, so much so that sometimes Maverick often had to rouse her from bed in the mornings.

Coupled with writing, Lilly's nightly browsing in the elderly couple's library soon absorbed almost an equal amount of time after she rubbed against a large book she remembered from the church house, but found it too hard to reach and too heavy to lift. Lilly informed Maverick that she required his expertise to bring the book down—it was too weighty and unwieldy for two mice. Composing her own book stopped for two nights while she assisted Maverick in the colossal enterprise (for mice) of preparing to take the book down. After two nights of engineering marvels orchestrated by Maverick, which proved as impressive as any of his deceased brother, and with all infants asleep, Lilly and Maverick Mouse eased the weighty tome off the shelf and then downward with the aid of skids and the book ladder, an infinite number of carefully arranged rubber bands at various angles, and their own biceps. The book came to rest on the library floor before it could be positioned for reading in a suitable space. Neither one had even little idea of how this book would mark out the rest of their lives, and particularly Lilly, even though Lilly and Geronimo had been privy to a scandal about the book when they lived in the church house.

"Where shall we start?" Maverick asked, as Lilly had a look of anticipation on her face.

"We shall start where it starts," Lilly said, as she cleared her throat and began to read.

She paused afterwards to indicate for Maverick the nature of the acrimonious debate she and Geronimo had heard at the church house over the legitimacy of this book for modern humans, many of whom thought themselves too advanced to subscribe to ancient myths. Though virtually all members of the congregation admitted it the bestselling book in the human world, the members at the church house soon fought over the advisability of retaining or banishing the book, with more voices in time opting for the latter. Eventually parishioner numbers declined to the point of making it necessary to sell the building and for the diminishing congregation to find a space elsewhere. Thus, the resisting few, beaten, found it necessary to undertake a migration, and with that, the migration of Lilly and Geronimo Mouse had begun.

Epilogue

"Word of this place first came handed down from previous generations. A few insist that one is not a rightful heir of the family unless they visit here at least once in their lifetime. I think Grandma Lilly said so too. Believe it or not, this building was once a church. Grandma Lilly always called it simply 'the church house.' Now it looks like anything but. If ever there was a matriarch of a family of mice, Lilly Mouse it was, hands down," Sylvester Mouse quipped to his bride of only a few days, Cynthia.

"Did she live here? How far back does she go?" she asked.

"Yeah, she lived here. At least a half dozen generations ago. She died something like nine years ago. She received no more substantial quantity of life than the rest of us mice, but word is that she did live a little more than two years. She and her mate, named Geronimo, didn't live here very long, but it was idyllic to them, and after they had to move from here, they continued to reminisce about their church house days. Some think Lilly always dreamed of returning to live here, but circumstances permitted no such wish to come to fruition. The couple did find another place to live, however, but in a wrecked car yard, and then, later, back into a house, which she described as quite splendid. Don't know anything much about that residence except she did like it, but I presume details are in her book. Geronimo died very soon after that move, and then Grandma Lilly married his brother."

"How do you know this?" Cynthia asked.

"Because Grandma Lilly put in a lot of details in her book, a book we think she wrote to record the lives of herself and Geronimo after they had to leave the church house. Some think she changed the perspective of the book after she and Maverick started reading the big book that they pulled off the shelves at the Tudor house. Nevertheless her own book was masterfully written and she worked to bring it right up to her death, and did. Some in the family who've had occasion to read some chunks of it say it rivals *I Climbed a Mountain*." Grandma Lilly was a reader and was always looking to tell a story and tell it well. And she read a lot for the sake of finding stories."

"She surely couldn't top Ephraim Mouse?" Cynthia mildly protested.

"Maybe not, but Ephraim is a mythical figure; the people in Grandma Lilly's book are earthlings, grounded and remaining in the dust of the earth as they look to heaven. I hear that is the way she put it in her book. By the way, we do know *I Climbed a Mountain* was her favorite book of all time—though I've heard she mentions it less and less frequently in her own book, I mean as one comes to the end. And in her book there is a deliberate detour to tell the story about a man hanging on a tree which she ran upon in the book she and Maverick pulled down from the shelves at the Tudor house. "

"They never put the owner's book back on its shelf?"

"I think they didn't have to, because no one in the house ever came to get it; so after a while Lilly and Maverick kept it on the bottom shelf for the ease of their own nighttime reading, without worry that anyone would notice the different placement of the book."

"But you still think she can best Ephraim Mouse?" Cynthia inquired.

"Maybe not, but she explains a lot, I mean about the family, but there is only one copy, I mean there are the actual pages of the book she wrote, and I hear it gets passed around a bit. I've never actually seen that book, but I know something of what's in it from others who have."

"Okay, but what didn't you know that she tells, I mean that you can remember?" Cynthia asked.

"That she and new husband Maverick had twelve children, and she names them in her book I'm told. Some that I remember are Isaac and Issachar and Naphtali."

"Unusual names."

"Yeah, and we don't know where she and Maverick got them, the names I mean though some in the family claim to know," he explained.

"What else?" Cynthia inquired, now intrigued by this family story.

"Well, from what others have told me, Grandma Lilly was most intrigued in the big book by the story of the man who hung on a tree. What captured her attention was the fact that the writings in the book that came after the record of that event insisted that this extraordinary man was not dead even after that, that being a thing called the crucifixion." Sylvester explained.

"Not dead after being dead?"

"Yes. And she thought if this were so, the mouse predicament might be overcome."

"I don't understand."

"The mouse predicament—that our life is so short, and comes to an end almost as soon as it begins and we can't do much about it. Grandma Lilly and son Issachar became obsessed with a plan to find this eternal man and any secret of living a life without end he possessed. She admitted such a thing sounded too fantastic, but she and Issachar would nevertheless venture to a place called Galilee and find this man and appeal to him for an extension on their lives.

"As Grandma Lilly began to draw up a plan of migration to Galilee for the two of them, she painfully began to realize that she hardly had enough life left to make such a long journey, much less a round trip, so she insisted that Issachar pick a younger brother and the two of them travel together, in the hope that one and maybe both could find this man before their own deaths, and that in sufficient time they could travel back to their family to relay any hopeful message.

"After the two departed and about six months later, Lilly died, too soon for her two traveling sons to return to her with any news. After another six months Issachar returned, but without his brother who had fallen overboard and into the sea on their return journey as stowaways. However, on the emotional reunion with his ten siblings, so the story goes, Issachar ventured to tell an astonishing story. This was the story of how and why the man had ended up hung on a tree and died as a result. But the extraordinary part of the story was that death had not snuffed out the life of the man, for he was proclaimed to be one who promised a life that did not end with natural death and that life after death could literally be forever, and that, because of his death."

"Sylvester."

"Yes?"

"I'm glad we came here today."

www.ingramcontent.com/pod-product-compliance
Lightning Source LLC
Chambersburg PA
CBHW071518150726
48000CB00002B/582